OUTRIDERS

EXPEDITION TO WILLOW KEY

ED DECTER

ILLUSTRATED BY SAMMY YUEN JR.

ALADDIN PAPERBACKS
New York London Toronto Sydney

Many thanks to:

Dr. Rebecca Shipe of the Department of Ecology and Evolutionary Biology at UCLA—any science that is accurate: hers; any that doesn't make sense: mine.

Dr. Benjamin Kendall, who has delivered thousands of babies and explored an equal number of coral reefs.

Jeff Folmsbee, for all things kayak.

Jon Messeri, for all things sailing.

Jen Klonsky, the world's best editor and most enthusiastic Outrider team member.

Barbara Marshall, a wonderful literary agent and friend to screenwriters everywhere.

Patrick Purdy, Boerne High School, thank you for your Spanish assistance.

And to Cheryl and Abigail, who make everything in life possible.

ALADDIN PAPERBACKS

An imprint of Simon & Schuster Children's Publishing Division

1230 Avenue of the Americas, New York, NY 10020

Text copyright © 2007 by Frontier Pictures, Inc. and Ed Decter

Illustrations copyright © 2007 by Simon & Schuster, Inc.

All rights reserved, including the right of reproduction in whole or in part in any form.

ALADDIN PAPERBACKS and colophon are trademarks of Simon & Schuster, Inc.

Designed by Sammy Yuen Jr.

The text of this book was set in Janson Text.

Manufactured in the United States of America

First Aladdin Paperbacks edition January 2007

10 9 8 7 6 5 4 3 2 1

Library of Congress Control Number 2006931468

ISBN-13: 978-1-4169-1306-1

ISBN-10: 1-4169-1306-8

For William F. Decter,
father, friend, Outrider

THE OUTRIDERS BLOG

BOARD NOT BORED

EXPEDITION: WILLOW KEY

Entry by: Cam Walker

Note: If some policeman or agent of the FBI happens to click on this website, please understand that my dad had no knowledge of the stuff that happened at Willow Key, and when he did find out about it he was absolutely not happy. Also, since I'm only twelve, it is possible I'm making all of it up.

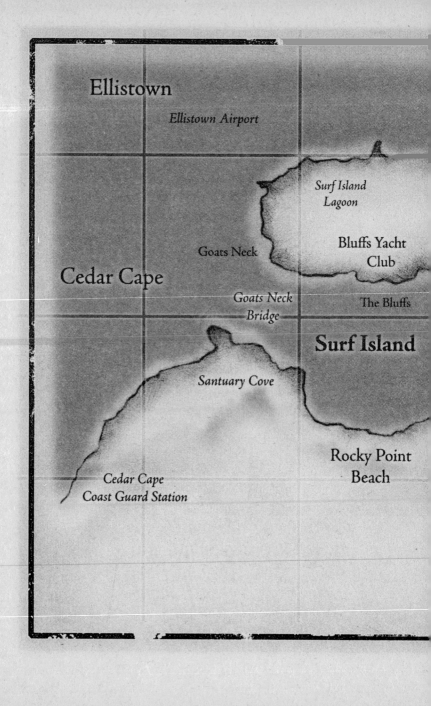

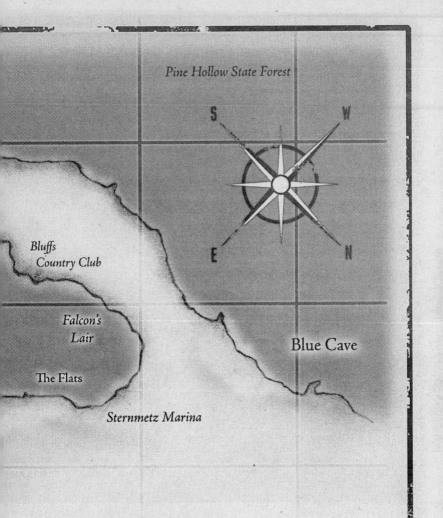

MAP OF SURF ISLAND

CHAPTER ONE: HARVESTING

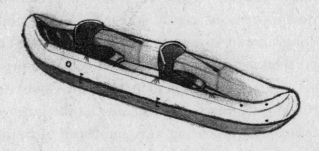

I was breaking every safety rule of scuba diving. I wasn't certified or even junior certified, which is what someone my age needs to be. I was diving at dawn in murky unfamiliar waters, and, worst of all, I was diving *alone*. The number-one hugest mistake you can make when you strap on a scuba tank is to go into the water without a diving buddy. You'd think that I would have been freaked out, but I wasn't. The only thing I was worried about was that someone might spot me, because I definitely shouldn't have been swimming in the water hazard that fronted the seventh green of the Bluffs Country Club.

Most of the members of the Bluffs Country Club are old—really, really old. There is a reason for this: It costs a ton of money to join the Bluffs, and on top of that the members don't just let "anyone" join. You have to be the "right sort" of person. So I guess if you want to play golf at the Bluffs it takes a long time to save up the money to join the club, and then it takes even longer to convince people that you are "member material." This must take around sixty years, because most of the guys who tee it up have hearing aids and those ultra-thick glasses that old dudes wear. I don't know much about golf, but I do know that guys who are really, really old have a tough time reaching the seventh green, which (according to a sign on the tee box) was 210 yards long. On the plus side, most of these ancient guys couldn't see or hear when their golf balls plunked into the water hazard in front of the green, which was why there were *thousands* of barely used balls resting at the bottom of the small pond just waiting to be harvested. Each used golf ball was worth twenty-five cents to Chuck at Surf Island Discount Golf and Tennis. So you can understand why golf ball farming was *critical* to fund the expeditions of the Outriders and why

I was scuba diving alone in front of the seventh green.

Well, I wasn't exactly alone. My friend Wyatt Kolbacher and I had scavenged two Bluffs Country Club golf carts, and he was hiding a few dozen yards away in the woods. Many years ago, when we were in fifth grade, Wyatt had made a breakthrough discovery that had revolutionized transportation for the Outriders. All golf carts are started with a small key. It was Wyatt who realized that all of the golf carts at the Bluffs used *the exact same key*. If you had a key for one of the carts, you had a key for them all. So, of course, each of us had our *own* key, which came in really handy when we needed to transport more golf balls than we could carry.

On a normal golf-ball-farming excursion Wyatt and I wouldn't bother scavenging two golf carts. We also wouldn't risk something as dangerous as scuba diving in a water hazard. We would simply harvest the balls that had zinged off into the woods (which, for some reason, the members called "the rough"), slip them into our backpacks, and then duck under the "guest entrance" we had created in the perimeter fence that surrounds the country club. From that point we would hook the backpacks to a trolley pulley that we had rigged to a zip line. The zip line connected the highest point in Surf Island—the Bluffs—with the lowest point—the Flats—where all of my friends and I lived. Once the backpacks whooshed down the zip line through the pine trees, they would end up at the Good Climbing Tree in my best friend Shelby's backyard. Shelby would climb the tree (she's ultra-gymnastic), unhook the backpacks, and store the balls in the "Ball Barrel." But this wasn't a normal day of golf ball farming. We had to finance a HUGE expedition (don't worry, I'll tell you about it later) so we needed to take even HUGER risks.

I had just finished filling up my fifth backpack full of balls when I heard a *plunk*. The plunking noise didn't sound like a fish jumping *out* of the water or a frog jumping *into* the water. It sounded like a golf ball landing very close to my head, and that's when I realized two things:

1. Golfers get up freakishly early to play golf.
2. I was going to be spotted.

Sure, I could have stayed underwater and hoped that the four elderly Bluffs members wouldn't spot a twelve-year-old scuba diving in the water hazard. But even though I wasn't certified or junior certified as a diver, I was experienced enough to read my compressed air gauge, which was very close to "empty." Also, even if I managed to avoid this foursome of golfers, there were sure to be more of them following close behind.

Even though the guys playing golf had those really thick old-guy glasses, they had no trouble spotting a kid in a wet suit, flippers, and scuba tank crawling out of the water hazard and onto the seventh green. I didn't know exactly how long it would take them to get into their carts and zoom the 210 yards toward me, but they did move a lot faster than I expected.

I yanked the scuba fins off my feet, picked up the backpack full of balls, and sprinted across the green into the woods where Wyatt was hiding. I could hear the angry golfer dudes jumping out of their carts and heading toward our position. I tossed the BC (buoyancy compensator) vest, mask, and fins into Wyatt's golf cart and then jumped into mine.

Wyatt could tell exactly what was going on by how fast I was moving. He could have said, "Wow, you set the all-time record for golf ball farming!" Or he might have said, "You are freakishly brave!"

But instead Wyatt chose to say, "I told you that last dive was one too many."

Wyatt has a peculiar talent for sometimes saying the exact thing you don't want to hear.

"We absolutely needed the golf balls," I said.

"We absolutely needed not to be caught."

It was hard to argue with the truth, so I just jammed my foot down on the accelerator pedal and rocketed the golf cart *right back toward the seventh green*.

One thing I can say for sure, the angry golfer dudes did not expect to see the trespassing kid in the wet suit blasting out of the woods and heading straight back *at them*. I could tell it didn't make any sense to the foursome, because they all froze for a few seconds trying to figure out how I could possibly be so insane as to drive *toward* trouble instead of *away* from it. Since they were still on foot, I zipped right through the frozen foursome, spraying them with pine needles. After that, they didn't stay immobile for long. All of them started yelling at the top of their lungs for me to stop (as if) and then scrambled toward their carts. But in the time it took for them to get their golf carts in gear, I was a few hundred yards down the fairway cruising toward the clubhouse.

One thing *I* didn't expect was for the guys chasing me to use their cell phones and call in reinforcements. I didn't actually turn around and see them make the calls. I just figured it out, because the next thing I saw was a squadron of golf carts rising over the hill just to the left of me. It kind of reminded me of one of those Xbox 360 games when you have just cleared a dungeon of a bunch of mutants and then you go through a doorway and there's like a hundred and fifty new mutants waiting to rip your head off.

You would think I would have employed some kind of evasive maneuver and tried to outrun the ten golf carts that were now chasing me. But I didn't do that. I kept heading straight for the Bluffs clubhouse. Once again, my odd strategy confused my pursuers. They had so expected me to veer *away* from them that some of them had *anticipated* my move and made turns in the direction they *thought* I was going. This caused a few of the golf carts to collide, and in the confusion I was able to jet ahead over a small rise where I could see the McGooghan Bridge in front of me.

The McGooghan Bridge, which, according to a brass plaque mounted on the handrail, was named after some Scottish guy who designed the course in 1803, was really narrow. It was only wide enough for one golf cart to go across at a time. If you were playing a normal round (and weren't being chased by twenty angry guys), you would tee off at the first tee right next to the outdoor patio of the Bluffs clubhouse, drive across the McGooghan Bridge, and head out to the first fairway. But I was now doing the exact opposite—I was careening toward the narrow bridge and planning to drive across it in the wrong direction.

The golfers chasing me must have been pretty amused at my choice of escape route, as I could hear them laughing. It was hard to blame them, as I could see a colorful wall of ancient golfers wearing pink and green pants, white-coveralled caddies, green-uniformed groundskeepers, golf course marshals wearing blue jackets, red-vested valet parkers, black-aproned waiters, and gray-shirted locker room attendants lined up on the clubhouse side of the bridge, just waiting for me to cross so they could capture me, bring me to justice, and ship me off to a youth authority work camp, where I would be wearing some kind of orange jumpsuit. But there were three things they all didn't know:

1. The backpack next to me contained no farmed golf balls, only crumpled-up newspapers.
2. By this time Wyatt had sent all five backpacks (which *were* stuffed with farmed golf balls) down the zip line.
3. I was never going to make it to the other side of McGooghan Bridge.

The narrowness of the bridge worked to my advantage. No one wanted to risk a head-on collision with a psycho kid in a wet suit, so everyone on the clubhouse side just held their position. The old and angry golfers behind me had now spread out and thought they were *herding* me toward the narrow bridge. I raced onto the fairway side of the bridge, and, since there was no possible way to turn around, the guys chasing me simply stopped their carts and waited so they could enjoy the show of me getting captured near the clubhouse. Halfway across, I skidded to a stop, and, without hesitating even a millisecond, I JUMPED OVER THE RAILING of the McGooghan Bridge.

I know, it sounds kind of Tom Cruise–like and dangerous, but the McGooghan Bridge is only about fifteen feet high and I knew *for sure* I was going to land in a soft grassy spot. I knew this because the day before I had scouted this escape route. That's why I chose that exact spot to hide the inflatable canoe.

The Bluffs Country Club is affiliated with the Bluffs Yachting and Beach Club. I only mention that because the Yachting and Beach Club was a deep resource for scavenging all types of nautical craft—like the inflatable canoe. Not many ultra-ancient dudes can paddle an inflatable canoe. But for some strange reason the members of the Y & B Club all own either kayaks or canoes. (They also own huge sailboats and motor cruisers, but that has nothing to do with my story.) I was pretty sure that the lawful owner of the canoe was probably one of the old guys yelling at me from the McGooghan Bridge but I was also pretty sure that the owner would never in a million years connect the bright yellow boat with something that he had bought and paid for. So I had scavenged the canoe, knowing full well I was going to return it after escaping down the Puerta River.

The Puerta River was more like a raging brown stream. But it was plenty big enough for the inflatable canoe to navigate. It was fast moving, particularly after a rain, and as soon as I pushed the yellow boat into the current, I was racing down the Puerta, leaving about fifty angry golfers and about the same number of country club staff behind me. I could hear their shouts echoing in the narrow granite ravine that held the Puerta. But the ping-ponging shouts became softer and softer as the current took me away from the country club.

I promise I'm not bragging, but my plan had worked really well. That's kind of what I'm best at— planning stuff. I'm not like one of those kids you read about who dreams up a scheme to link up a bunch of computers and find a way to win at Internet poker (really happened), but when it comes to figuring out a way for the Outriders to go on cool expeditions and get the gear we need, I'm ultra-good. Which is why I was so surprised when the waterfall came up on me so quickly.

Of course I *knew* about the waterfall. What I didn't know was how strong the current just above the falls could be. I had planned to navigate the canoe to a calm section of the river created by an enormous fallen pine. But now I realized my canoe and I had whipped past the small inlet and no amount of paddling on my part was going get me out of the churning rapids that were funneling me directly toward the falls.

I feel really comfortable on fast-moving water. I surf. I surf a lot. So it wasn't like I was panicking. In fact my mind was clear and clicking through all my possible options:

1. Jump out of the canoe.
2. Stay in the canoe.

Unfortunately both option one and option two had the same end result: I was going over Puerta Falls. I made a split-second decision to stay in the canoe. A few months back I had tried diving off some cliffs (not huge ones like you see on ESPN). I came out of one of my dives and landed a little more horizontal than vertical. And it hurt—really badly. So my thinking was that the bright yellow boat was *inflatable* and my body was *not*—so I thought I'd let the canoe absorb as much of the impact as it could stand. Also—and this proved to be faulty reasoning on the part of my brain—I thought that if I was *in* the canoe with my paddle, maybe there was some way for me to *navigate* down the falls.

Here's an important thing to remember if you

ever find yourself in a similar situation: An inflatable canoe falling over a waterfall tends to act like a sail and lift the boat AWAY FROM THE WATER and into the AIR.

So none of my surfing or paddling experience was going to come into play; I was free-falling and, most frightening of all (I'll admit I was now ultra-scared), the canoe *folded* in half and I was swallowed in a yellow cocoon of polyvinyl fabric. I couldn't see or hear a thing. I didn't know if I was going to land in the crash pool of the waterfall or splatter against the boulders that ringed the pool. For some reason Wyatt's voice popped into my head. His voice said, "The plan wasn't so good after all."

Wyatt's voice disappeared as soon as I heard the explosion. Well, it wasn't really an explosion; it was the sound of the inflatable canoe smacking into the crash pool and rapidly DEFLATING. The next thing I knew I was deep underwater, tangled in the now-limp yellow canoe and struggling for a way to claw myself out of the wreckage and make it to the surface. Picture putting a roll of quarters inside of a napkin and throwing it into the water; the napkin would fold up around the quarters and sink straight to the bottom. I was now the roll of quarters and the deflated boat was the napkin.

I remembered Wyatt showing me a movie about US Navy SEALs. In one of the training scenes, the SEALs get dunked upside down in a deep pool. Their super-tough drill instructor tells them to follow the air bubbles to the surface. That seems like a really terrific survival technique, especially in a swimming pool where you can see the bubbles. But here in the deep, dark depths of the crash pool, I couldn't see any bubbles. Not one bubble. But, like I said, I'm at home in or around the water, so I did finally claw my way out of what was left of the yellow canoe and find my way to the surface. I then took the biggest inhale of fresh air my lungs could hold. Apparently, at some point I must have been screaming, because I needed to take in a lot of air.

About now you must be wondering, were the golf balls really worth it? The answer is no, but the expedition to Willow Key absolutely was. I guess I should tell you why we wanted to go to Willow Key so badly. It had to do with our biology teacher, Mr. Mora. He is trying to become a doctor—not the medical kind, but the scientific kind. He is working really hard nights and weekends to get a PhD in biology from Ellistown University. In order to get this thing (he sometimes calls it a "doctorate"), he needs to do a bunch of research. He is in the middle of this project called a "biomass study" down at Willow Key. Apparently a biomass study is when you take a sample of water or dirt and count how much living stuff there is in it. If it is dirt, you may be counting how many worms or bugs you find, but with water you might be counting big stuff like fish or frogs, but also small stuff like algae and tiny microscopic animals and plants. That's the kind of biomass study Mr. Mora wanted to do in Willow Key—the water kind. He wanted to see how pollution in the water was affecting Willow Key, which, if you saw a picture of it, looks a lot like the Everglades in Florida.

Just to be clear, I'm not some kind of science freak. Last semester I cruised to a solid B. I mean, biology and stuff is sort of interesting, but not the kind of thing I stay awake at night thinking about (like surfing).

The reasons I wanted to go to Willow Key were:

1. I've never been farther than fifty miles from Surf Island.
2. It would absolutely be a cool expedition.

3. We owed it to Mr. Mora. (This should have been number one.)

MR. MORA

A lot of people talk about doing good stuff for the environment, but Mr. Mora really walks the walk. He recycles, he uses solar energy at his house, he rides a bicycle—he doesn't even own a car. But he's not one of those guys who is all in your face about it. Mr. Mora is always teaching how stuff is *connected*— not just the whole little-fish-get-eaten-by-bigger-fish deal, but how a tiny thing like throwing your chewing gum on the street can cause a bird to choke and the bird dies, and it might be a mother bird and then her chicks die, and then there is less food for the owls and then the owls die, and then there are no predators to eat the rats and so you get like a billion rats, and then the rats cause all these diseases and people start getting sick—all because you littered instead of putting your chewing gum in the trash. I know that example seems a little exaggerated, but still, things like that stick in your brain. And just like he cares about the ecology and stuff, Mr. Mora cares about *us*.

I don't want to seem super-harsh about the other teachers at Surf Island Middle School, but not one of them cares as much as Mr. Mora. A few of the teachers are really nice, some cut you slack if you didn't get all your homework finished, and a few go easy on you if you're on the basketball team. But most of the teachers at our school are kind of *disappointed* that they ended up at Surf Island Middle. They would have preferred to score a job at Overlook Prep up in the Bluffs. Overlook is one of those private schools where you can live in a dormitory. (They call it a "boarding" school, but to me that sounds like a place that teaches surfing.) Overlook has a huge gymnasium that seats like five thousand people, a separate auditorium with a digital sound system and ten science labs with computer workstations installed at every desk. I know all of this for a fact because I have often visited Overlook Prep, just not during "official" school hours.

Our facilities at Surf Island Middle aren't as high end as the Overlook campus. For example, our gym flooded a few years back and all the wooden floorboards are warped. If you try to dribble a basketball, the ball zings off at weird angles. Our basketball team (I'm the point guard) has adopted a "pass-only" offense, which attempts to completely eliminate dribbling. This strategy has won us a lot of home games, as none of the opposing teams are prepared for the ball ricocheting sideways and rolling out of bounds as soon as it makes contact with the gym floor. So I can't really blame the teachers at Surf Island Middle for wanting to work someplace that isn't so "warped." Most of the Surf Island teachers apply for a job at Overlook *every single year* and then spend their time wishing and praying that there might be a teaching vacancy (which there never is). That's another reason Mr. Mora is so cool—he actually got *offered* a job at Overlook and *turned it down*.

Mr. Mora never explained to us why he didn't take the job at Overlook, but I have this theory. Well, it's not all scientifically tested out or anything, so I guess it's more of a "belief." I think Mr. Mora felt that he had made a commitment to building the biology department at Surf Island Middle School (in fact, he *was* the biology department) and if he left, there would be no one to teach biology at all. This combined with the fact he'd have to wear a collared shirt and a tie up at Overlook Prep convinced him to turn down the job. After he said no to Overlook, you would think the other teachers would have really admired Mr. Mora, but I think the rest of the faculty started to view him as some type of loser, someone who wasn't smart enough to appreciate the tremendous opportunity he'd been offered. We watched the other teachers walk past Mr. Mora in the hallways and refuse to make eye contact with him. It was like he had spit on their dreams and so they were sort of "spitting on him."

Of course this just made us (Mr. Mora's students) like him even more. He hadn't given up on Surf Island Middle School and he hadn't given up on us, so we would have followed him anywhere. Oh, and another cool thing about Mr. Mora: He saved Wyatt's life.

Before I tell you what happened to Wyatt you need to know something about Wyatt's brain. But before I tell you about Wyatt's brain you need to know something about Wyatt's parents, Morgan and Betty Kolbacher. Mr. and Mrs. Kolbacher were BOTH in the navy. Now they run Surf Island Salvage at the very tip of Sternmetz Marina. Morgan and Betty's salvage yard is piled with weird-looking hunks of stainless steel, copper, brass, aluminum, titanium, teak, oak, mahogany, glass, Plexiglas, hemp, and nylon from every imaginable scow, dinghy, runabout, sloop, tugboat, catamaran, ferry, tanker, and tender that ever floated on water. The strangest thing was that Morgan and Betty not only knew where to find any bizarre fitting or cog that someone was looking for, they actually spent all of their spare time reading manuals and catalogs about all of that marine-type stuff. Their office at the salvage yard and their house were FILLED with sailboat parts catalogs, ship propeller charts, and even military diesel engine repair manuals. I don't think Mr. and Mrs. Kolbacher even owned a book of fiction. So from the moment Wyatt was born, he was surrounded by thick booklets with titles like *Stevenson's Guide to Jib Sheet Cleats, Modern and Antique*. Mr. and Mrs. Kolbacher would always brag that even before he could read, Wyatt would sit for hours staring at the pictures of marine hardware in their catalogs.

I don't know much about the human brain, but I think all those catalogs kind of molded the way Wyatt's mind works. Wyatt (who we sometimes call the King of Gear) sort of sees the world broken up into pieces that he can classify. For instance, Wyatt is obsessed with dirt bikes, specifically motocross motorcycles. He can tell you in detail the differences in compression, gear ratio, and torque between the

Honda 450R and the Yamaha YZ450F. It's not like Wyatt could actually ride one of those bikes (which is a good thing because Wyatt is not that coordinated), but he's loaded with information about a massive amount of stuff—which is why, of everyone in the Outriders, Wyatt loved biology. There was a world full of animals, plants, and microscopic organisms, and all of them had their own classifications. They all fit somewhere in a huge catalog of living things, and Wyatt's mind had to know where everything fit. So that's why Wyatt ended up doing an extra-credit biology project and lit himself on fire with two-hundred-proof ethyl alcohol.

It's not important to know what the project was about or why Wyatt decided to do it; what is important to know is that two-hundred-proof ethyl alcohol is not just flammable, it is *ultra-flammable*, and when it catches on fire, THERE IS NO FLAME. Here's the strange thing about fire: A medium-hot fire is orange, a really hot fire is blue, and for some reason a wicked-hot fire is CLEAR. Wyatt discovered this the hard way when he was working on his project in what Mr. Mora calls the "biology lab" (which is just a normal classroom with desks), and Wyatt began to detect a really noxious odor. He also noticed a strange sensation that he described as "a scorpion stinging my head with lava-hot venom." But it was Mr. Mora who realized that Wyatt's hair was on fire. Mr. Mora had noticed "heat diffraction waves" emanating from Wyatt's head, and that, combined with the distinctive aroma of burning hair, convinced him to spring into action and grab a red metal canister from the wall and douse Wyatt's head with fire-extinguishing foam. Mr. Mora immediately pushed Wyatt's head into a sink basin and rinsed the foam out of his hair. He then broke off several leaves from an aloe plant and rubbed the gooey sap onto Wyatt's head to soothe any burns to the scalp. Wyatt was okay, and miraculously his scalp didn't get any serious burns. But unfortunately half of Wyatt's hair had completely vaporized. Wyatt had a full head of healthy hair in the front of his head, and was virtually bald on the back half. It was as if it was Halloween and he had put on a clown's wig backward. Once we knew Wyatt was okay, the rest of us found his new hairdo our friend Bettina's parents' beauty shop, the Cut Hut, to get Wyatt's hair situation stabilized. Wyatt left the Cut Hut with a new Shaquille O'Neal–style head shave and an undying loyalty to Mr. Mora.

So that's why if we could raise enough money for the field trip, we were all going with Mr. Mora to Willow Key to do a biomass study. Of course the humongous amount of money we needed to get to the wetlands proved to be less of a problem than the bunch of really nasty people who were trying to make sure that we would never leave Willow Key.

But I'm getting ahead of myself.

CHAPTER TWO: FUND-RAISING

"**A** polyvinyl patch and marine glue."

These were the first words Wyatt spoke to me after my hundred-foot drop over Puerta Falls. He might have said, "I'm so glad you're alive!" or "That must have been the scariest ride ever!" But apparently Wyatt was more concerned with the two items we needed to repair the inflatable canoe.

"Do your parents have that kind of stuff at the salvage yard?" I asked.

Wyatt didn't even bother to respond, the question was so insulting. Mr. and Mrs. Kolbacher had *everything* nautical at Surf Island Salvage.

The reason Wyatt was so focused on repairing the canoe is that we absolutely *had* to fix it. If we replaced the boat in tip-top condition (except for the polyvinyl patch and marine glue), that was considered SCAVENGING, and that was okay. But if we didn't fix the canoe or didn't return it, that was considered STEALING, and that wasn't okay. The yellow inflatable had to be seaworthy and back at the Yachting and Beach Club by the end of the day. That was the unwritten law of the Outriders and we stuck to it (usually).

So Wyatt and I decided to stow the canoe in a hollow tucked underneath a thicket of bushes. Actually it was a thicket of poison sumac, which kind of guaranteed that nobody would come poking around and find the canoe before we got to fix it. A few months back I had discovered the poison sumac the hard way. A bunch of us had been searching for an abandoned well. That might seem like a strange thing to do, but there's this local rumor that everyone in Surf Island has heard about: Apparently, before the Revolutionary War, some Spanish pirate hid gold doubloons or jewels or something near the town. I don't take the rumor too seriously, but if I hear about an abandoned well, I have to check it out—

you know, just in case. We never found the well, but I *absolutely* found the poison sumac, which is kind of an evil plant because it violates that old rule of the forest: "leaves of three, let them be." Sumac has *seven* leaves, so you really have to know what to look for. I don't know much about plants, but I do know that if by mistake you stick your head into a poison sumac bush looking for an abandoned well, you will wish that you had been stung by two hundred thousand jellyfish instead. That's how bad the rash is. So I was being ultra-careful not to touch any part of the sumac bush while hiding the canoe.

"You guys hit the mother lode," Shelby said as she ran up the path that snaked through the woods from her backyard. Shelby is almost always moving at high speed. She's my best friend but she is tough to keep up with sometimes. "There are almost a thousand golf balls—" Shelby stopped short when she saw the deflated canoe. "Explain." When something interests Shelby, she needs information fast.

"I thrashed it," I said.

"Tree?"

"Waterfall."

"Ni-ice," she said, which is like the highest Shelby compliment.

You'd have to know Shelby as well as I do to realize she was also a little *jealous*. When cool stuff happened, she liked to be doing it instead of hearing about it. Maybe that's why she stepped close and aikido-flipped me to the ground.

You would think this is strange behavior, but I'm kind of used to it. Shelby is good at many things, and aikido is just one of them. I don't know much about how aikido is different from the kung fu stuff you see in movies, but the flip move seems pretty much the same.

"You're supposed to be ready," Shelby said with a smile.

"You're supposed to be normal," I said to her as she helped me to my feet.

"Normal bites. Now, let's go. We've got a barrel of golf balls to sell." Shelby turned and ran back toward her house. For some strange reason, I never liked to let Shelby get too far ahead of me, or even get ahead of me at all, so I sprinted to catch up. Wyatt is kind of small and wiry, so his legs are a lot shorter; he lagged behind.

When we broke from the woods into Shelby's backyard, our friend Ty was already leaning against the trunk of the Good Climbing Tree next to the

Ball Barrel. I was relieved to see that he had brought the Gator. You should know that a lot of this story is about Ty and ultra-intense secrets we learned about his past, but I'll get to all that stuff later. You're probably wondering about the Gator.

The John Deere company is famous for making tractors, but they should really be famous for making Gators. Wyatt classifies the Gator as a "utility vehicle," but that classification doesn't do it justice. If you were a hundred yards away from a Gator, it would look similar to one of the golf carts we scavenged up at the Bluffs Club. But once you got closer you'd notice some very important differences. First of all, it is painted a very cool John Deere green and has yellow seats. Second, it is gasoline-powered and has all-wheel drive. Third, it can go anywhere and do anything; it is the King Kong of utility vehicles. And here's the coolest thing: Ty's Gator wasn't just the standard model; it was the *high-performance* Gator, the HPX 4x4.

I guess, technically, the Gator didn't belong to Ty. Mr. Dyminczyk, Ty's father, works for the Town of Surf Island Water Department (TOSIWD), and so, technically, the Gator belongs to them. But when Mr. Dyminczyk was working and using his

TOSIWD-issued Ford 350, which he nearly always was, the Gator belonged to the Outriders.

Our HPX 4x4 was outfitted with a brushed-aluminum flatbed, which made it look as if a golf cart and a small pickup truck got married and had a baby. The Gator was the absolutely perfect vehicle for this part of the plan because we needed something heavy-duty enough to carry the Ball Barrel (which was now completely full of golf balls) to Surf Island Discount Golf and Tennis.

Ty glanced down at his watch. Ty doesn't say much, hardly anything at all. That bothered our teachers and a lot of other adults, but we were all kind of used to it.

"I had some problems with the canoe," I said.

"Must to hurry." When Ty did speak, everyone tended to really listen.

I'm not sure how much a thousand golf balls weighs, but I can tell you it is a lot. The weight of the ball-filled barrel had caused it to sink into the ground a few inches. The plan was for Wyatt, Ty, and me to wrestle it into the back of the Gator. Wyatt and I were kind of limbering up like Olympic weightlifters when we saw Ty squat down, yank the Ball Barrel out of the ground and casually set it on the flatbed of the utility vehicle. You would think Wyatt and I were surprised, but we weren't. Ty is the biggest kid in our grade. He's even bigger than most of the kids in the high school and stronger than any of them. It's possible Ty isn't twelve years old. No one really knows. Way back in fourth grade, he and his father came from this Eastern European country that isn't on the map anymore, or maybe is on the map but has a different name. Anyway, Ty didn't speak English when he arrived, and neither did his dad. He just sat down in our classroom one day and became the biggest and strongest fourth grader in the history of Surf Island. I promise I'm going to tell you all this other important stuff about Ty, but first I need to say something about driving a Gator without a driver's license.

MY THOUGHTS ON DRIVING A GATOR WITHOUT A LICENSE

I'm not sure if there is a law that says you need to have a driver's license to operate a utility vehicle. I actually don't want to know. My feeling is this: If you worry about every single rule and regulation that is out there, fun stuff will pass you by. Driving a Gator HPX 4x4 is fun. If you get a chance to drive one, go for it.

CHUCK'S DISCOUNT GOLF AND TENNIS

The only thing we couldn't do was drive the Gator on the main roads (especially Surf Island Boulevard)—not because of the no-license thing, but because the TOSIWD and Mr. Dyminczyk didn't know we were scavenging their utility vehicle.

The great thing about Surf Island is that there are so many shortcuts and paths through the woods that it is never necessary to get on a main road. The four-wheel drive of the Gator easily handled the rough terrain as we slalomed through the forest that ran parallel to Surf Island Boulevard. I secretly wished I had been driving the HPX 4x4 when the golfers were chasing me in the morning.

Ty was nice enough to let me drive the Gator while he sat in the passenger seat. Shelby and Wyatt were riding on the flatbed, holding on to the Ball Barrel, making sure it didn't tip over. In about seven minutes we pulled into the rear parking lot of Surf Island Discount Golf and Tennis. The Fund-raising Expedition had worked pretty well up until this point (except for the plunge over the waterfall). But I have to admit, the next thing I had planned was something that I wasn't really proud of.

I had arranged for our friend Bettina to meet us at

Surf Island Discount Golf and Tennis. That wasn't the thing I was ashamed of. I had made Bettina promise to make sure that her older sister Viveca drove her to Chuck's. I know that doesn't sound really bad, but . . . well, you'll see.

Chuck, who owns Surf Island Discount Golf and Tennis, is about sixty-five. He very rarely ever shows up at the store. He is usually out fishing. Chuck's son, Chuck Jr., really runs the business. He's in his forties. But Chuck Jr. rarely makes contact with actual customers. He's usually sitting in his tiny, cramped office, on the telephone, and arguing with some golf club or tennis racket distributor. If you walk into Chuck's and want a racket strung or a sand wedge regripped, you had to see Chuck Jr.'s son, Charles.

Charles is about nineteen and is working his way through Gull Bay Technical College. I think he is studying to be an air-conditioning and heating repair engineer. Charles is really skinny and has this huge Adam's apple jutting out from his neck. It kind of looks like Charles opened a can of tennis balls, swallowed them, and had one get stuck in his throat. Lots of people make fun of Charles behind his back, but not us. Charles is the guy who pays us for our golf ball farming. He is the closest thing the Outriders have to a banker. If a golf ball was in perfect shape, it was worth twenty-five cents. If it was dinged up a little, it was worth a dime. Charles inspected each and every ball very closely. He didn't own the store, but he took his job very seriously.

But the main thing you need to know about Charles is that just like every other guy sixteen or older on Surf Island, he dissolved into a puddle of goo in the presence of Viveca Conroy.

Of course Viveca had no idea that she was being used as a fishing lure to reel in a better price on the golf balls from Charles. She just thought she was going to pick up a bunch of Bettina's friends and take them to the car wash. (I'll explain all about the car wash later.) Viveca wasn't especially kind or generous about giving Bettina rides. But Bettina and Viveca had a very efficient sister-to-sister understanding. Viveca would occasionally provide automotive transportation. In return, Bettina would remain silent on the unusually active and clandestine social life of her older sister. Did you ever see those movies where an army ranger gets captured behind enemy lines and is then tortured for information but absolutely refuses to give up the position of his unit? Bettina is like that army ranger.

Nothing Mr. and Mrs. Conroy could throw at their youngest daughter could make her crack. So as long as it didn't interfere with something important like a date or a trip to the mall, Viveca would ferry some of us around in her old Camaro convertible.

Charles was starting to pick through the Ball Barrel so he could sort the dinged-up golf balls from the pristine ones, when Bettina entered the store—followed by Viveca. Wyatt, Ty, and I watched as Charles looked up and his eyes locked on Viveca. Charles swallowed hard, which made his huge tennis-ball-size Adam's apple bob up and down. You would think that Viveca's dark mocha-colored skin, thick cascading waves of brown hair, and light green cat-like eyes were the things that caused all the older guys to act like idiots. But it wasn't just Viveca's looks. After watching her for all these years, I finally figured out what it was: her smile. Viveca had these really white, straight teeth. When she saw someone she knew (which was everybody in town), Viveca's eyebrows would raise just slightly, and then, a fraction of a second later, the sides of her mouth would bend upward causing her lips to part just slightly, revealing those really white, straight teeth. It was as if her expression said, "I was just thinking about you!" In reality, Viveca thought almost exclusively about herself, but the rest of the world, and most importantly Charles, did not know that.

As soon as Viveca approached the counter, Charles lost the power of speech. All he could manage was to continue swallowing hard. It looked as if there was a tennis match going on inside his neck. This was the reaction we had expected from Charles, so Bettina turned to her sister and said, "Viveca, you know our friend Charles, right?"

Realizing that he might soon be engaging in a conversation with Viveca, Charles got very pale. The tennis ball in his neck stopped moving, and I realized that he was no longer breathing.

"Of course I know Charles," Viveca said. And then she unleashed her smile.

Charles flinched and began blinking involuntarily as if someone had thrown salt into his eyes. He tried desperately to speak but could not push any sound up past his Adam's apple. This was our moment.

"Hey, Charles, we have to get over to the car wash. Can we settle up on the golf balls?" I said.

It took a moment for Charles to remember that there were other people in Surf Island Discount Golf and Tennis beside Viveca. When he came back from the far-off land in his imagination where he and Viveca were walking along Rocky Point Beach holding hands, he almost seemed grateful to me for allowing him the opportunity to get back to business and show everyone how good he was at his job.

Without looking at the Ball Barrel, Charles said, "Well, these all seem to be in pretty good shape. Do you have an accurate count?"

"Nine hundred and eighty-eight," Shelby said. "I counted them twice."

"So at twenty-five cents a piece, that's two hundred and forty-seven dollars exactly." Charles smiled in the direction of Viveca. He had done the calculation in his head and believed he had a chance of impressing her.

Viveca lowered her chin slightly and looked up at Charles through a lock of dark wavy hair. "Wow, that's a lot," she said, then unleashed a *second smile*. Even if Viveca had known the exact reason we'd asked her to the store, she couldn't have helped our cause in any greater way.

Charles managed a weak smile and even tapped his forehead with his finger, as if to say *There are more rapid math calculations where that came from*.

Never in the history of mankind was a guy behind

a counter at a golf shop so *exhilarated* and so *eager* to hand over 247 dollars to a customer. I pocketed the cash and then said, "Thanks, Charles. We gotta head to the car wash. We're late. You gonna swing by with the truck?"

Charles hadn't taken his eyes off Viveca. "Sure, yeah, yes, okay," was what he said. I don't think he had even heard the question.

Bettina, Shelby, Wyatt, Ty, and I then followed Viveca back toward the door. I didn't turn back to look, but I was sure Charles had not taken his eyes off Viveca until she reached her Camaro in the parking lot.

After we had all piled into the convertible and were cruising down Surf Island Boulevard, Ty leaned down toward me and whispered, "Is not good. What you did."

Ty was right. Charles had always been good to us. It wasn't like we were technically *cheating* him—we did deliver 988 golf balls, but not all of them were twenty-five-cent golf balls.

Shelby always has an eerie sixth sense about what I was feeling or thinking. She spoke in a low voice so that Viveca couldn't overhear. "Relax. Charles will remember this day for the rest of his life. And if we want to get to Willow Key, we need to raise a lot of cash, and fast. We've got to focus on the car wash."

Shelby, as was usually the case, was right. The 247 dollars was a ton of money, but it wasn't nearly enough to get our biology class to Willow Key. That's why we weren't counting on golf ball farming to solely fund the expedition. Our main source of income was going to be the car wash.

I can't take credit for inventing the idea of holding a school car wash to raise funds for a field trip. Students all across the world do the same thing every weekend. The idea I *can* take credit for is the Surf Island Middle School Mega-Wash.

The concept behind the Mega-Wash is very simple. At a normal car wash at a middle school, drivers usually just stand around and wait for ten or fifteen minutes until their car is hosed off, and then they drive away. The drivers feel really good that they donated five bucks to whatever cause the students were raising money for. The Mega-Wash was designed to maximize cash flow during those critical ten to fifteen minutes that the driver is stranded without a motor vehicle and waiting to get back into his car. All of the Outriders and most of our parents had been working for weeks to come up with highly profitable entertainment and refreshments that would be offered to the waiting drivers. We wanted them to kill time by spending money.

I got the Mega-Wash idea from a magazine article about a computer gaming convention that was held in Las Vegas. One of the game designers said that he hoped that all of the conventions would be held in Las Vegas because he liked to play slot machines *at the airport*. I personally have never been to an airport or flown on a plane, but I assume waiting around in an airport is a lot like being in detention—you would be pretty hungry for something to amuse yourself and you would be willing to pay money to do it.

THE MEGA-WASH

In order to advertise the Mega-Wash we needed a sign, so my dad got to work and I really think he outdid himself. I should mention that my dad has his own sign company. Actually, it isn't really a company, it's just my dad. He designs, manufactures, and installs the signs himself. Dad made two signs for the Mega-Wash. He pointed out that if we wanted to maximize business we needed a sign for drivers headed in both directions on Surf Island

Boulevard. When it comes to signage (and only sign-age), my dad knows what he's talking about. So, as Viveca approached Surf Island Middle School, my friends and I got our first look at my dad's handi-work. The sign was beautiful, really colorful, with clear, easy-to-read letters. It read: IF YOU DON'T GO TO THE MEGA-WASH, IT MEANS YOU HATE CHILDREN.

I know it seems kind of harsh, but if you think about it, no one wanted to be the kind of person who hated children, so they *had* to pull into the car wash.

Dad was a pretty busy guy, so I was really grateful he'd given us a hand. He can get really enthusiastic about stuff like a field trip. Dad hasn't traveled too much in his life. When my mom left (long story), he had to raise my older brother, Kyle, and me all by himself. So if one of his sons got a chance to do something cool like go on a biomass study in a swamp, my dad was all over it. When I first told him Mr. Mora was thinking of taking us to Willow Key, my dad said, "You have to go. It could be a pivot point in your life." I think he meant to say a "piv-otal" point, but his way made just as much sense. When I told him that we had to raise a humongous amount of money before we could go on the field trip, he said, "I got you covered on the signs." My dad wasn't a super-hero or anything, but he was a man of action. And his signs were working—there were a lot of cars in the parking lot of Surf Island Middle School.

It had taken a lot of time and effort to plan the underwater golf ball farming and put together the Mega-Wash, but our hard work seemed to be paying off. A triple row of cars was lined up in the semicircular driveway in front of the school. This was designated as the WASH AREA. Drivers were not permitted to be in their cars (see plan above) and were instructed to wait in the cement courtyard directly in front of the school. This was the area that we secretly referred to as the KA-CHING ZONE, but our customers knew it as the WAITING AREA.

Here's just a few of the cash-generating enterprises we had going at Mega-Wash:

1. A QUALITY CAR WASH: This is the key to any successful automotive cleansing venture—you want your customers driving away from the experience saying to themselves, "Wow, my car really sparkles." A quality

wash stimulates word-of-mouth advertising. This seemingly obvious business principle is surprisingly overlooked at many middle school car washes, but not at the Mega-Wash. Mrs. Kolbacher had rummaged through the inventory at Surf Island Salvage and brought along something called a high-infusion nozzle, which was a cone-shaped brass attachment that turned a normal garden hose into a turbo jet of furious, unbridled aquatic power. Mrs. Kolbacher personally took command of a ragtag clump of middle school kids and whipped them into a finely tuned platoon of car washers. We only charged five dollars for the car wash (six dollars for pickup trucks). This barely covered the cost of automotive detergent and interior car treatment. But my dad had explained to me the concept of a "loss leader." He told me that on Thanksgiving a supermarket will sell turkeys for a dollar. The supermarket knows that their shoppers will come for the one-dollar turkeys, but have to buy stuffing, potatoes, and pies before they leave. Our plan was to lure customers into the Mega-Wash with the low-priced car wash, and then have them spend real money in the ka-ching zone.

2. AUTHENTIC THAI CUISINE: My friends Din and Nar Bonglukiet (it's okay if you call them the Bonglukiet twins) are originally from Thailand. Their parents, Tran and Lin Bonglukiet, run a small market called Surf News. Since there are always around ten or twelve of Din and Nar's cousins staying at the Bonglukiet home, Mrs. Bonglukiet is really accustomed to cooking for large groups of people. And since most of the Bonglukiet cousins are from Thailand, Mrs. Bonglukiet cooks a humongous amount of authentic Thai food every day. Din and Nar managed to convince Mrs. Bonglukiet and several of the cousins to set up plastic folding tables in order to sell Thai entrees ranging in price from three dollars (tum yam soup) to six dollars (Penang curry with shrimp). Additionally, Din and Nar had brought along their dog, Howie. (Howie goes wherever Din goes.) I mention this only because Howie is a 243-pound mastiff and he is very noticeable wherever he

goes. If you have never seen a mastiff, try to picture a Saint Bernard. Now try to picture a Saint Bernard with a light tan coat and black muzzle. Now picture duct-taping two Saint Bernards together. Then you would have a mastiff. It was Nar's idea to put a tiny saddle on the back of Howie and offer "mastiff rides" to children two and under. On a normal day Howie doesn't move very much. But Nar is a self-described "dog whisperer" and assured us all that Howie would obey his commands.

3. NOVELTIES: Mrs. Ruiz (Shelby's mom) worked for a realty company in town (the kind that makes you wear those mustard-colored jackets). She had cajoled the corporate offices of the realty company to donate Surf Island Realty pens, Surf Island Realty maps, and Surf Island Realty flashlight key chains for sale at the Mega-Wash. Since she had obtained all this merchandise at zero cost, any sales we made were pure profit that would go toward the expedition to Willow Key. Mrs. Ruiz had far too busy a work schedule to actually sell the novelties, so Shelby was put in charge of sales. Shelby

had also invented something that she called the "Five-Dollar Chocolate-Chip Cookie," which was a Toll House cookie the size of a hubcap. Shelby used her awesome algebra skills to determine that each cookie only cost fourteen cents to make. (She did not include the cost of natural gas in the Ruiz oven or the wear and tear on the Ruiz cookie sheets; these costs were hidden in the overall Ruiz household operating budget.) We planned to net four dollars and eighty-six cents on each gigantic cookie. Shelby experimented with a "Ten-Dollar Chocolate-Chip Cookie," but its size exceeded the width of a normal baking oven.

4. THE DUNK TANK: You've all seen this contraption. There's a huge tank of water, a tiny little seat, and a target that you hit with beanbags. If the beanbag scores a bull's-eye, whoever is sitting on the tiny little seat gets dunked in the tank. For some reason, this attraction is the most popular and profitable at every county fair. Somehow, some way, Shelby had convinced her father, Mr. Ruiz, to man this concession. Mr. Ruiz was the most

dreaded teacher at Surf Island Middle School (he taught Spanish), and although he had won two Teacher of the Year awards, we knew that every single student would like to take a shot at dunking him. Normally Mr. Ruiz wouldn't *ever* go for being plunged into a tank of water, but when it came to his daughter Shelby and furthering her education by helping her go on a field trip, he would put himself through any humiliation. Shelby's little sister, Annabelle, was going to be on hand to provide a steady stream of dry towels to her dad. If we put Annabelle on the dunk tank seat we would be millionaires. Lots of people in Surf Island, particularly anyone who had ever babysat her, would like to see her dunked in a tank. Unfortunately Annabelle would not consent to sit on the dunk seat because she has an aversion to being agreeable. She's a very strange six-year-old. (For more about Annabelle, see my blog about our trip to Blue Cave.)

5. THE MEGA-WASH KIDS' SALON: Mr. and Mrs. Conroy (Bettina's parents) had graciously volunteered to open a satellite Cut

Hut at the Mega-Wash. They were donating their services and supplies. Mr. Conroy would cut kids' hair. Mrs. Conroy would do face-painting for kids. We were very excited about this venture. Little kids' hair doesn't take long to cut (their heads are very small) and all children (especially girls) love to get their faces painted. (For some reason cat noses and whiskers were the most popular.) We wanted parents to have a place to park their kids so they would have to spend even more time in the ka-ching zone. We had hoped beyond hope that Viveca would have wanted to help her parents at the booth. Just her presence would guarantee the arrival of every male high school student and his car. But Viveca needed the day to break up with one boy so that she could replace him with another who had a much "hotter" car.

6. SurfFreeze CONCESSION: Mr. Flores, who owned Island Freeze (the food shack which was the official meeting place for the Outriders), had agreed to bring his SurfFreeze machine. A SurfFreeze is a kind of Slurpee

drink that is a local favorite in Surf Island. Mr. Flores is also the employer of my older brother, Kyle. It was Kyle who would be manning the SurfFreeze machine. This was not a purely for-profit enterprise, as we were splitting the proceeds with Mr. Flores. Because we needed to maximize profit, I was forced to assign Wyatt to watch over Kyle. I love my brother, but he was prone to giving away free beverages to his friends. Mr. Flores was constantly frustrated with my brother's lack of ambition. On this day I was taking a small walk in Mr. Flores's shoes.

7. THE PETTING ZOO: Mr. Mora was blown away by the scope and magnitude of what we had planned. He very much wanted this field trip to happen, so he had gone to extraordinary lengths to call in some favors and bring something special to the Mega-Wash table. Mr. Mora had some biologist friends at the Ellistown Zoo, and they had agreed to allow some exotic snakes and lizards to be showcased in a special petting-zoo exhibit. The centerpiece reptile that was making the trip to

Surf Island Middle was Sinzia, a thirteen foot-long reticulated python. Apparently *sinzia* is the Swahili word for "sleepy," which, when you have a petting zoo, is exactly what you want a thirteen-foot python to be. Mr. Mora was the perfect person to be the ringmaster of a reptile petting zoo because he knows more stuff about animals than anyone I've ever met. Did you know a squirrel will pee on his own fur to make himself smelly and disgusting to a predator? At the Mega-Wash our customers could pet a python and learn something about the animal kingdom at the same time. We felt the profit potential for this venture was unlimited.

Ty's dad was working, but even if he didn't know it, he had donated the Gator. My dad had kicked in the signs. So in one way or another, all of the Outriders and their parents had pitched in to make the Mega-Wash a spectacular, humongous event.

But it wasn't.

In fact it might have been the most drastic failure in the history of middle school fund-raising.

At first, just a few small things went wrong:

1. A normal person can't eat a chocolate-chip cookie twice the size of his head.
2. Authentic Thai food is very spicy—much too spicy if you are not authentically Thai. This hurt sales.
3. Nobody wants to pay for anything that has a Surf Island Realty logo because they know they can get that stuff for free.
4. For some reason people will pay for a haircut in a barbershop but not out in the open air.
5. Kids enjoy face painting at *parties*. They don't expect it at a car wash and therefore reject it.
6. Very few people, except some odd little boys, want to pet a reptile.
7. Students do not want to dunk a teacher who likes to give detentions.

I considered most of these small setbacks "learning experiences." If a friend of mine were thinking of running a car wash, I would gladly pass on my wisdom about these tiny mistakes as "lessons learned." But the apocalypse that followed was not something that anyone could have anticipated.

At first I blamed the heat. It was sunny and warm, which are the ideal conditions for a car wash. But as the morning turned into midday, the sun got much stronger. Remember I told you that the ka-ching zone was located on the cement area in front of the school? This was a mistake. White cement reflects heat. In fact, and I'd have to check this with Mr. Mora, I think white cement *amplifies* heat. So by noon, the ka-ching zone was not a place anyone wanted to be. (If you are planning a similar type of event, find a grassy area and camp out there. Bring sun umbrellas if you have them. Trust me, I learned this stuff the hard way.) Another thing about light-colored cement is that it amplifies *light*. Everyone, even those people lucky enough to bring sunglasses, had to squint. Several customers became so disoriented that they wandered back into the wash area and almost got run over by incoming cars. So the *one* area that we wanted our customers to spend the most time in had become the most torrid, unforgiving, and hostile environment for a human being, much like the way scientists describe the surface of Mercury.

Customers and Mega-Wash workers began to get woozy. This wooziness caused a lot of poor judgment and triggered a series of chain reactions, which will be talked about at Surf Island Middle School until the end of time.

Reptiles are cold-blooded. That means that their circulatory systems can't regulate their own body temperature. They rely on the environment to provide a temperature suitable for their species. Snakes, for instance, like it warm, so if the temperature drops, you will find a snake sunning himself on a rock. But snakes don't like it *too* warm. If the sun gets too strong, a snake will naturally seek shade, or even retreat into a hole. But Sinzia the thirteen-foot gray-green reticulated python didn't have a hole to retreat into. Here on the surface of Mercury, Sinzia was almost FRYING. Mr. Mora began to panic. He not only loves all the animals of the world and wouldn't harm any of them, but he also couldn't think how he would explain to his biologist friends at the Ellistown Zoo that he had FRIED their python. Mr. Mora yelled to Mrs. Kolbacher that he needed water immediately. Betty Kolbacher turned around to find Mr. Mora hoisting an enormous but very limp reptile in his arms. Wanting only to save the life of the animal, Mrs. Kolbacher aimed the nozzle of the hose in the direction of Mr. Mora and the snake. She had apparently forgotten that the high-infusion hose attachment produced such a ferocious surge of water (we found out later the US Navy used these nozzles to clean barnacles off of battleships) that several side-view mirrors had been blown off the customers' cars. Her lapse in judgment, clearly due to the heat, became apparent when Mr. Mora and the snake were propelled backward a full fifteen feet, both of them crashing into the Bonglukiet's Thai food concession.

A few bad things happened at once. Sinzia did not like the high-powered spray of water or the fall on top of Mr. Mora (or perhaps the too-spicy Thai peanut-oil salad dressing), and the sleepy snake woke up—*really* woke up. It began to coil and writhe frantically, trying to get away from the danger it felt it was in. The snake weighed over a hundred pounds, so it inflicted a lot of damage on the Thai food concession, tipping over the table, the cooking pots, and all of the food Mrs. Bonglukiet had prepared. Then the screaming began.

Mrs. Bonglukiet was not screaming in frustration or anger that Sinzia had destroyed all of her beautifully prepared food. She was screaming in utter terror. Apparently Mrs. Bonglukiet had an unnatural fear of snakes, believing all to be either poisonous or evil. Technically Sinzia was a constrictor and therefore did not *bite*, but Mrs. Bonglukiet was not fully schooled in herpetology or had some sort of bad childhood experience with reptiles, because she *screamed and screamed and screamed* as if she was actually being swallowed by the snake.

There is one other thing you need to know about Mrs. Bonglukiet: She feeds Howie. Sure, Howie is Din's dog, but when Howie eats, it is Mrs. Bonglukiet who puts down the food. That means a lot to a dog, and particularly to Howie, who, due to his massiveness, needs to be fed a lot. So when the very slow-moving Howie heard Lin Bonglukiet *screaming* he came *running*.

A further complication was that a two-year-old girl named Bunny Atwell was at that time sitting in the small saddle on top of the 243-pound mastiff. Just seconds before Mrs. Bonglukiet had started to scream, Din had been tugging on Howie's collar just to get the mastiff to take a few steps and give Bunny a ride. Now Howie was *rampaging* toward a thirteen-foot gray-green reticulated python with revenge in his eyes. Bunny Atwell now also began to scream.

I bet you would imagine that a screaming toddler riding atop a huge dog who is determined to rip apart a gigantic writhing snake would have been the low point of the Mega-Wash, but you would be wrong. That's because you don't know about the bees.

The ka-ching area was so mercury-hot that Mr. Flores's SurfFreeze machine could not produce sufficient refrigeration to make the drinks icy. That means that the Day-Glo colored mixture was just a tepid, gooey, sloshy batch of *sugar water.* So when Howie rammed against the SurfFreeze machine on his way to kill the snake, the large vat of SurfFreeze mixture exploded on the hot cement, sending a tidal wave of blue-raspberry sugar water surging across the ka-ching area.

There was one positive by-product of Howie's collision with the SurfFreeze machine. For a brief instant, Howie's momentum toward the python was slowed. In that brief moment, Kyle was able to pluck Bunny Atwell off of the tiny saddle and cradle her in his arms. (Kyle's alert thinking made him something of a local hero for a few weeks.) Even though Bunny was now safe, Sinzia was not. Howie was charging forward like a runaway semi-truck. Then Mr. Mora made another mistake.

For some reason, Mr. Mora decided to *pick up the snake.* Mr. Mora is really, really smart, but this just goes to show you that the heat combined with all the disasters threw off the reasoning of even the smartest guy at the Mega-Wash. I guess, in the moment, Mr. Mora thought he could lift the heavy snake out of harm's way. His strategy could have worked if Howie had been a Chihuahua, for example, but, while on all four legs, Howie's enormous head is level with a grown man's chest. If Howie decides to rear up on his hind legs, he is taller than any human alive. Mr. Mora realized this, but too late. Howie was locked in on the python much like an F-18 fighter tracks an enemy plane. So when Mr. Mora attempted to clean and jerk the snake above his head, like some sort of really bad weightlifter, Howie didn't hesitate for a second. He JUMPED. But he jumped *late*.

If Howie was a more active dog, he would have had a lot more practice leaving the ground. But because he is essentially sedentary, he is rusty in the jumping department. Howie's overall laziness is what saved Sinzia's life. Had Howie jumped in the proper spot, he would have been able to spring to the level of the snake and clamp his hugely powerful jaws on to the snake's body. But Howie jumped too close to Mr. Mora, which meant that Howie's paws, which must have weighed eighty or ninety pounds each, rammed into Mr. Mora's STOMACH. Normally that would have knocked Mr. Mora *down*, but Howie's leaping trajectory knocked Mr. Mora *up*, and Sinzia the python, who was now coiled around Mr. Mora's arms, went *up* with him.

Some deep-seated survival instinct must have told the snake to release its grip. As Mr. Mora crashed into Mrs. Conroy's party makeup table, the intrepid python uncoiled itself and flew about eight feet through the air, landing with a tremendous SPLASH in the dunk tank.

A lot of kids find Mr. Ruiz ultra-harsh as a teacher. To be honest, I'm not very fond of Mr. Ruiz. It might be because Shelby's dad doesn't like *me* very much, because he thinks I'm "dragging his daughter down into mediocrity." But despite my feelings, I did not wish for a thirteen-foot gray-green reticulated python to get tossed into the dunk tank next to Mr. Ruiz.

Shelby's dad isn't a coward, but I have never seen a human being scramble out of a tank of water as fast as he did. He reminded me of one of those dolphins you see on the Discovery Channel leaping out of the ocean. Sinzia the snake had no interest in harming or attacking Mr. Ruiz. The python was only interested in keeping its head above water. (Don't worry, snakes can swim.) In a few moments, Sinzia found the small dunk tank seat and began to coil around it. Now that the python was far away from Mrs. Bonglukiet and she was no longer screaming, Howie completely lost interest in tearing the snake apart.

Mr. Mora had the wind knocked out of him, but he was able to get to his feet. There was a cloud of powdery makeup surrounding him. He looked like he was some sort of baker who'd decided to jump into a vat of flour. But he was alive and undamaged. Howie trotted over and began licking his face, almost as if to say, *I didn't mean it*. My biology teacher was okay, and Sinzia the snake was a little scared, but alive and well. You would think the apocalypse was over. But you forgot about the bees.

By this time a swarm of the angriest, most determined bees that seemed to only exist in order to suck up spilled SurfFreeze mixture descended on the kaching zone. Little kids hate bees, parents of little kids hate bees, and the rest of humanity just doesn't want to get stung. What happened next can only be described as mass hysteria. Everyone ran. MegaWash workers ran in every direction away from the middle school. Customers ran to the safety of their cars. They jammed the vehicles in gear and zoomed out of the parking circle, leaving only rectangular squares of dry asphalt where their cars used to be. About a minute later, there was no one left standing in the ka-ching zone except me and Mr. Mora.

I wanted to escape from the bees, but I seemed to be frozen in place. Not out of fear, but out of shock. I had totally and absolutely failed to pull off the Mega-Wash. Even worse, I had totally and absolutely failed to come through for Mr. Mora. I couldn't blame the heat for what had happened. It was me. I don't know what I had been thinking. It is hard to raise even a little bit of money. We had needed humongous amounts of cash. There was probably no way on earth we could have amassed enough of it to go on the field trip. Clearly nobody should trust me to organize anything ever again. Maybe kids from the Flats don't even merit cool stuff like biomass studies in Willow Key.

Mr. Mora, still looking very baker-like coated in white makeup, was carefully pulling Sinzia off the dunk tank seat. I hustled over to try and help him. Mr. Mora looked over at me.

"It's amazing what you pulled together. I'm really proud of you," he said.

"You're joking, right?"

"Most people talk about things they'd *like* to do. You and your friends just *do* them. I admire you."

Mr. Mora had caught me off guard. All I could manage to say was, "At least *you'll* still get to go to Willow Key."

Mr. Mora just smiled as he pulled Sinzia to safety. But he didn't say anything.

"You still get to go, right?"

Mr. Mora looked down. "I can't do the biomass study alone. You guys weren't just coming along for the ride. I really needed the help."

I thought the apocalypse was bad, but this was worse.

"But you could still go down there, find some people to help you."

"There's no way I could afford that." Sinzia had now coiled around Mr. Mora's body as if to hug him. Mr. Mora saw the expression on my face. "Cam, it's my job to worry about you, not the other way around."

A bee stung me. I barely even felt it. In fact I was glad I had been stung; I had just ruined my favorite teacher's life. I deserved worse.

"Wow, that's a big car," Mr. Mora said.

I turned and saw a long, black, Rolls-Royce limousine glide into what used to be known as the wash area.

"You don't see many of those in this town."

Mr. Mora was right. Surf Island was not a Rolls-Royce kind of town. There was only one person who owned a Rolls-Royce, Mr. Chapman Thorpe—and when the smoked-glass window lowered on the rear door, that was who I saw.

"Hello, Cam."

I should mention that I knew Mr. Thorpe and he knew me. It's a really long story, but I had returned something very valuable to him and he had helped me out of a tight spot. I wouldn't say we were friends, mainly because I wasn't sure what Mr. Thorpe was all about. And, to be honest, I was afraid of him.

"Um . . . hello, Mr. Thorpe."

"Chappy."

As if I was going to call him by his nickname. I just stood there staring for a few seconds while Mr. Thorpe's chauffeur opened the rear door. Mr. Thorpe didn't get out because something was wrong with his legs and he had to walk with these weird-looking aluminum crutches.

"Wouldn't it be polite to introduce me?" Mr.

Thorpe looked in the direction of Mr. Mora.

"Oh, right. Mr. Thorpe, this is Mr. Mora."

Then Mr. Thorpe extended his hand to Mr. Mora. They shook. "It is a pleasure to meet you, Peter."

Peter is Mr. Mora's first name. But I hadn't *said* his first name. See, this is what I mean about Mr. Thorpe: He always keeps you off balance. I got the distinct feeling his arrival was not an accident, but I decided to say, "Would you like your car washed, Mr. Thorpe?"

Mr. Thorpe almost smiled. His Rolls couldn't have been more gleaming if it had been coated with shellac.

"Actually I'd like to invite you both up to Falcon's Lair."

Falcon's Lair is Mr. Thorpe's mansion. It has no address, just a name.

Mr. Mora looked down at his makeup-coated body. "I don't think I'm in any condition to go anywhere."

"I think you'll want to come. It's about your field trip to Willow Key, if you are still interested in going."

Mr. Mora's expression was a mirror of mine. We both looked shocked, as if for no reason someone had just slapped us on the face with a raw salmon.

For just a moment I thought that this was all some type of dream, like the heat had caused me to hallucinate or the bee sting had caused a swelling of my brain. But when the chauffeur opened the other rear door, I found myself following Mr. Mora into the limousine and sitting across from Mr. Chapman Thorpe.

My father would have said that this could turn out to be a huge "pivot point" in my life. And it was.

CHAPTER THREE: NEGOTIATING

"This all started because of a woman."

Mr. Mora and I had no idea what Mr. Thorpe was talking about. We were seated on one side of an ancient dark wooden desk. Mr. Thorpe was seated across from us. His aluminum canes rested against the rear glass wall of the solarium. Don't be too impressed that I knew we were in a room called a "solarium." I'd been to Falcon's Lair before. You should know that Mr. Thorpe's estate is HUGE and crammed full of stuff from the olden days, which Mr. Thorpe calls "antiquities." Last time I was in this room Mr. Thorpe explained that he collects all of these "artifacts of history" because he has an "insatiable curiosity" about the past. Mr. Thorpe must have been the most curious guy on earth, because the antiquities swallowed up every square inch of available space in the humongous stone mansion; it was like the past was squeezing out the present. My thoughts on the subject got interrupted by Mr. Mora, who was clearly trying to figure out why we had been summoned to Falcon's Lair.

"Excuse me, Mr. Thorpe, but *what* started with a woman?"

"The rivalry."

"Which rivalry?"

"The one between Commodore Sternmetz and Alvaro Bautista di Salamanca."

I only recognized the name of Commodore Sternmetz. He was some British naval dude that the Surf Island marina was named after. I could tell Mr. Mora was getting a little frustrated. He was supersmart and logical and wasn't used to Mr. Thorpe's technique of toying with people's minds. Before my teacher could ask his next question, Mr. Thorpe raised a single finger as if to say, *Wait just a moment*.

Mr. Thorpe opened a drawer of his desk, pulled out a small framed drawing, and put it down so that

Mr. Mora and I could take a look at it. You could tell the wooden-framed drawing was really, really old, like something you would see in a museum. The picture was of a woman dressed in some type of old-fashioned gown. Her dark hair was pulled up with a fan-shaped thing, which stuck out of her head like the fat side of a pizza wedge. (I don't know much about stuff girls put in their hair.) The woman's expression was very strange; she was sort of looking off into the distance like she would have rather been anywhere else in the world than posing for the artist who was sketching her. I looked up at Mr. Thorpe. I had a very specific list of questions in my mind:

1. Who was this woman?
2. How did she fit into Mr. Thorpe's story?
3. What did any of this have to do with Willow Key?

As if reading my brain waves, Mr. Thorpe said, "All your questions will be answered, Cam." Then Mr. Thorpe smiled, which is kind of freaky because he's super-old and his teeth are long, so his smile looks more like a grimace. "Perhaps I should show you the ship's log and the map."

Now more questions popped into my head:

1. What ship?
2. What log?
3. What does any of this have to do with Willow Key?

Mr. Thorpe put an old leather-bound book on the desk. It was about the size of a paperback novel. He also pulled out an ultra-old map . . . well, actually a *piece* of an ultra-old map that was preserved between two sheets of clear plastic. Mr. Mora and I now had three things to look at: the drawing of the woman, the old leather-bound book, and the piece of the ancient map. I just didn't know *why* I was looking at them. I was in that land beyond confusion. I felt myself getting sleepy, as if my brain was shutting down to avoid overheating.

Mr. Thorpe's bright blue eyes were sparkling. I think he was *enjoying* my confusion. He raised one of his age-stained hands and pointed at the drawing of the woman.

"Her name is Dona Juliana di Castillo. Not much is known about her except that she caught the eye of a young British naval officer named Sternmetz."

Finally, like a train slowly pulling out of a station, Mr. Thorpe's story started moving forward.

"But Dona Juliana did not return Sternmetz's affections. She was in love with a brash young Spaniard named Alvaro Bautista di Salamanca, who was better known as El Trueno."

"The train?"

Mr. Thorpe sighed, probably wishing I'd paid more attention in Spanish class. "*El trueno* means 'the thunder,' and he was Europe's most notorious pirate."

At the mention of the word *pirate*, my brain jump-started awake. "Wait a minute—does this have something to do with the legend about the Spanish gold buried somewhere in Surf Island?"

Mr. Thorpe seemed pleased that he had penetrated the dense fog of my understanding. "Yes, it very much does."

"You mean that legend is *true*?" Mr. Mora asked.

"That's what I'm trying to find out and why I need both of your help."

I sat up straighter. This was getting intensely interesting.

"Legend has it that El Trueno would approach a merchant ship under the cover of darkness. He'd then use a catapult to launch a flaming keg of gunpowder into the air. When the gunpowder exploded, it created a thunderous fireball. This would so startle those on the merchant ship that they barely noticed El Trueno's men taking over their ship. Almost no blood was shed on any of his pirate raids. When Sternmetz discovered that Dona Juliana's heart belonged to another, and that her beloved was the dreaded pirate El Trueno, Sternmetz vowed to capture the scoundrel and hang him."

Mr. Thorpe's butler, Giorgio, arrived with a plate of cookies and some tea. We thanked him, but Mr. Mora and I couldn't even think about refreshments. We were too engrossed in the three-hundred-year-old story.

"Dona Juliana discovered Sternmetz's intention to capture El Trueno and risked her life traveling from her home in Barcelona to his secret hideout to warn him. Dona Juliana had no way of knowing that she was being followed by Sternmetz and his crew and leading them directly toward the pirate. She also had no way of knowing that El Trueno was at that moment back in Barcelona stealing all the treasures from Dona Juliana di Castillo's family home and setting sail for the New World."

I found myself looking down at the drawing of Dona Juliana. Maybe she was thinking about El Trueno and his horrible betrayal while the artist was sketching her.

"Various historical accounts claim that a few months later Dona Juliana died of a broken heart."

"What happened to El Trueno?" I asked.

"Sternmetz pursued him across the Atlantic and chased him for years, but each time El Trueno managed to slip away. Finally Sternmetz set a trap and captured the Spanish galleon of El Trueno, but his quarry was not aboard. Sternmetz searched the ship from top to bottom. He was unable to find Dona Juliana's family fortune but he did find"—Mr. Thorpe looked directly at me—"El Trueno's golden sextant."

"Excuse me, hold on." I actually stood up, that's how confused I was. "When I was in sixth grade and you gave our class a tour of your house, you yourself told us that the King of England gave that golden sextant to *Commodore Sternmetz*!"

"And that's what I believed, until recently, when I came into possession of this." Mr. Thorpe pointed to the leather-bound book in front of him. "El Trueno's ship's log. Many passages refer to a golden sextant and describe it exactly. The log also gives clues about Dona Juliana's treasure and contained this section of a map."

Mr. Mora and I now took a closer look at the map fragment that had been laminated in plastic. The ink and paper were very faded and yellow-old, the writing was all curly-cue and in Spanish, but there was one thing we both clearly recognized: the northern half of Surf Island.

Surf Island isn't really an island; it is technically a peninsula. On the southern tip of town, a thin strip of land called Goat's Neck connects Surf Island to the rest of the coast. The town itself is sort of shaped like a football. The map fragment I was looking at was half a football, as if someone took a knife and sliced across the fat part of the ball. I could make out the locations of Rocky Point Beach (where I surf), Sternmetz Marina, and the Bluffs Yachting and Beach Club (which was founded by a grandfather of Mr. Thorpe). Obviously none of these places existed when the map was made, but there was no doubting that this was an ultra-old map of my home town.

This had been a very strange day. I'd gone scuba diving in a water hazard, been chased by angry golfers, kayaked down a river, flown over a water-fall, watched a mastiff with a toddler on its back try to kill a thirteen-foot reticulated python, and been stung by a bee, but sitting here with Mr. Thorpe in his solarium hearing a three-hundred-year-old treasure story was the freakiest thing yet. I looked at Mr. Mora. I just knew he was wondering the same thing I was, so I said, "This is all super-interesting, Mr. Thorpe, but—"

"Why are you here?"

"Because you invited us."

Mr. Thorpe sighed again. I guess he was frustrated I wasn't keeping up. "You're here because I want you to dive the wreck."

"The wreck?"

"The wreck of *L'Esperanza*."

Mr. Mora seemed to be following. "*L'Esperanza* was El Trueno's galleon?"

Mr. Thorpe fixed his hawk-like gaze on Mr. Mora and nodded as if pleased to be dealing with someone closer to his own level. "This ship's log suggests there may be more clues about the location of the treasure still aboard the galleon."

"But what does the wreck of *L'Esperanza* have to do with Willow Key?" I asked.

Mr. Mora turned toward me. "My guess is that the ship sank near Willow Key."

"That's right, Peter." Mr. Thorpe tapped on his skinny legs. "And I'm not in any condition to make the dive myself."

Mr. Mora seemed to be debating something inside of his head. Finally he said, "I'm sorry, Mr. Thorpe. The kids in my class are *twelve* and—"

Mr. Thorpe didn't let Mr. Mora finish. "*L'Esperanza* is in only twenty-five feet of water—it's not even a decompression dive." Mr. Thorpe now looked directly at me. "Not much deeper than the water hazard in front of the seventh green."

Mr. Mora had no idea what Mr. Thorpe was talking about, but I certainly did. I had shielded my favorite teacher from some of the details surrounding the fund-raising for the expedition. As always I was freaked out by Mr. Thorpe's intimate knowledge of the comings and goings of the Outriders. He was like one of those chess grandmasters who thinks twenty moves ahead, and I was like a guy with a bag of marbles playing Chinese checkers.

Mr. Thorpe now swiveled his gaze back to Mr. Mora. "Why so worried, Peter? You'll be diving with your students. Afterward you can complete the biomass study. You need it for your doctoral thesis at Ellistown, don't you?"

I knew Mr. Mora pretty well and I could sort of read his body language. For instance, when the Surf Island Board of Education had considered cutting costs by removing all the computers from our school, Mr. Mora's jaw got really tight and his eyes narrowed slightly. My biology teacher had that exact look at this moment. Mr. Thorpe may have been a grandmaster in chess, but Mr. Mora did not like being a pawn.

"Cam may know you, Mr. Thorpe, but I do not. I don't appreciate—"

I put my hand on Mr. Mora's arm to stop him. I don't have a clue why I thought I could handle this situation better than my teacher, but maybe it was because I had spent a little time with Mr. Thorpe and kind of understood how he operated. That didn't make me any less scared of him, however.

I looked directly at Mr. Thorpe and tried to pretend I was playing poker with my friends in the Outriders. "Are you offering to send us down there?"

"With all the equipment you need for the dive."

"And we'll have time for the biomass study?" I said.

"I'll fund it entirely," Mr. Thorpe replied.

"All we have to do is make the dive and see if we can recover whatever it is you're looking for?"

"That's all."

"And if we don't find anything?"

"Then so be it."

Some of his anger had subsided, but Mr. Mora still wasn't convinced. "Mr. Thorpe, with all due respect, we can't—"

"Refuse your offer," I said.

"Cam Walker . . ." Mr. Mora was using his "teacher voice."

I didn't let him get rolling. "Mr. Mora, I screwed up the Mega-Wash. I ruined your chance to do the biomass study. Mr. Thorpe is offering to completely bail us out. And on top of everything else, we get to dive a sunken Spanish pirate ship and help solve a three-hundred-year-old mystery of buried treasure. You're the smartest teacher I know, Mr. Mora. Do the math."

There was a long silence as Mr. Chapman Thorpe and I waited for Mr. Mora to weigh all the moral, teacher, and legal issues surrounding the decision. Finally he turned to Mr. Thorpe and said, "The board of education won't allow us to use any of their buses."

"I will fly you and your students to Willow Key."

"The plane tickets will be very expensive."

"Not to worry. You can use *my* plane."

"Your *plane*?" Mr. Mora said. (You have to understand, if you live in the Flats, it doesn't occur to you that someone you are speaking with may own an *airplane*.)

"You can take my seaplane. There is no landing strip near Willow Key for my jet."

Mr. Mora and I took a beat to digest this last bit of information. Apparently, from the sound of things, Mr. Thorpe had a jet AND a seaplane.

I broke the silence. "Mr. Thorpe?"

"I told you to call me Chappy."

"Um . . . there are twenty kids and Mr. Mora going on this expedition. How many trips back and forth do you want your seaplane to make?"

"Just one."

"But—"

"It's a big seaplane."

CHAPTER FOUR: EMBARKING

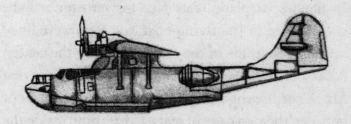

It *was* a big seaplane.

Technically it was a "flying boat." At least that is what Wyatt told us they used to call the PBY Catalina during World War II. Like I told you, I have never been on any kind of airplane, but I have seen TV shows and movies of people riding in them. The PBY Catalina looked nothing like anything I've seen before.

First of all, it was old—the one we were flying in was built in the 1940s. (Mr. Thorpe's pilot, Bobby, told us that.) The wings jutted out from the *top* of the "fuselage," which is the body of the plane, and had four propellers instead of jets. Behind the wings there were two huge windows that jutted out from each side of the plane's body like the eyes of an enormous bug. These windows let a ton of light flood into the cabin, so it was really bright inside. In movies, airplane seats face forward toward the cockpit. But in the flying boat, the seats were lined up along each side of the fuselage, facing the center. All of our backpacks and the diving equipment that Mr. Thorpe sent along were strapped to the floor between the two rows of seats. Everything inside the plane looked like it hadn't changed since the 1940s; the seats were covered in this thick, rough olive-green fabric that looked like an old army jacket. If you ever get to go on an expedition to a far-off location, I absolutely suggest taking a PBY Catalina; it lives in a land beyond cool.

I'm not sure what it sounds like inside a jet, but the cabin of a PBY Catalina is LOUD. You almost have to shout to talk to someone sitting next to you. I think the loudness contributed to all the weirdness that almost ruined the trip and broke apart the Outriders.

I'm still trying to sort out exactly what happened, but all I can figure out is that the weirdness started because of one tiny question.

We had just gotten all the gear loaded onto the PBY. Besides the Outriders, there were twelve kids from our biology class along for the expedition. I should also mention that Howie the mastiff was very comfortably camped out in a space between a pile of buoyancy compensators and our supply of air tanks. Bobby the pilot had started the engines and the propellers were roaring away. I was all amped up to get going on the expedition. As I sat down in one of the seats, I realized that I had been so excited when I woke up that I had forgotten to eat break-fast. I was thinking about how good a slice of pizza would taste. (I think this thought very often.) Ty was already sitting down in the seat to my right. There was an open seat on my left. And that's when I'm pretty sure the weirdness happened.

THE WEIRDNESS

Just as Shelby was about to sit down next to me, Bet-tina, who was right behind Shelby, said, "Oh, so that's how it works? You automatically get to sit next to Cam?"

Now remember, that's only what I *think* Bettina said. I'm not sure because of the engine noise and me dreaming about pizza.

Then Shelby got a strange look on her face and said, "Chill, Bettina. Whatever."

So Shelby moved all the way down the center aisle and sat between Din and Mr. Mora. Then Bettina sat down next to me.

No big deal, right? But for some reason, it was.

Wyatt, who was sitting across the center aisle facing me, is very alert to danger. Like I said, he's kind of small and skinny, so I guess he needs keener radar than the rest of us. Now remember, I am sitting there thinking about pizza, not realizing any weirdness has occurred. But when I looked at Wyatt, his eyes were huge, like something scary had just happened. I kind of tilted my head like a dog hearing a strange noise and Wyatt flicked his eyes in the direction of Ty.

I looked over at Ty (his real name is Timor, by the way) and he was staring forward, not looking at anything at all. Normally this wouldn't be alarming, since Ty rarely spoke—he mostly watched what was going on and thought his own private thoughts. But this was different. I got the impression that Ty was trying *not to look at me* as if *I had done something to make him angry*. I rapidly ran through a mental checklist of my recent interactions with Ty. When

I first saw him on the tarmac earlier that morning, I had said, "Hey, how's it going?" Since that time, I hadn't said a word to my friend, which was not unusual because of his perpetual quietness. But maybe on this particular morning Ty had wanted to have a more prolonged conversation and felt he had been snubbed.

The last thing on earth I would ever want to do is hurt Ty's feelings by not including him, so, as the plane rumbled down the runway and took off, I yelled, "How cool is this?"

And Ty didn't answer me. He just stared straight ahead looking at nothing. Now I was really, deeply confused. So I thought I would try again.

"How psyched are you to dive that wreck?"

Again, Ty didn't answer. I looked back at Wyatt. Wyatt gave me a look as if to say, *I told you there was a problem.*

As the plane angled up through a cloud bank, I was forced to recheck my mental checklist. I was certain nothing had happened earlier in the morning. Ty had nodded when I'd said hello to him, which was standard procedure in our friendship. So something must have happened since we got on the plane, but the only thing that had happened was the thing about Bettina wanting to sit next to me.

Then it dawned on me: The thing with Bettina and the thing with Ty's anger could possibly be connected! On the day when Ty first arrived at Surf Island Elementary, Bettina had lent him a pencil. That single act of kindness made a deep impression on Ty, and since that time it had become clear to all of us that he would gladly lay down his life for Bettina. One time when Bettina was practicing her archery at Goat's Neck Park, a group of older kids came by and swiped her bow and arrows. They started shooting the arrows all over the place (not a safe thing to do, by the way) and refused to give the bow back to Bettina. The next thing these older kids knew, Ty was charging toward them like some sort of rampaging bull. In about three seconds they found themselves on the ground and Bettina had her bow and arrows back. I hadn't thought about this incident for years, but now it seemed important. Did Ty think that Bettina wanted to sit next to me because she was crushing on me? And was he not speaking to me because he thought I was crushing on her? The idea was so ridiculous that I immediately pushed it out of my head. It had to be something else. I just had no idea what.

Suddenly I felt Bettina's hand touch my face. I flinched.

"What?"

"You had an eyelash.

"Oh."

I glanced to my right. Ty's face hadn't moved a millimeter. Maybe when we got to Willow Key, I would get a chance to find out what was bothering him.

"You think there'll be a reward?" Bettina said over the roar of the engines.

"A reward for what?" It was the strangest feeling, but I was uncomfortable talking to one of my best friends.

"For finding what Mr. Thorpe is looking for."

"Our reward is right here." I motioned to the PBY and all the gear.

Din said, "You mean Mr. Thorpe gets to keep all the treasure for himself?"

"Mr. Thorpe couldn't care less about the treasure," I said.

"Yeah, I'm sure," Shelby said with kind of an angry edge to her voice.

"You've been to Falcon's Lair. Mr. Thorpe has more ancient stuff than he could sell in a hundred lifetimes.

You think this treasure, if it even exists, would make a difference to him one way or the other?"

"So why does he want to find it so bad?" Nar asked as he was bending over and petting Howie.

"I think he wants to solve the mystery," I said.

"All of a sudden you're like the *expert* on Mr. Thorpe? You and he are *buddies* now?" Shelby almost hissed when she spoke.

"Hey, what's with you?" It was like all my friends had gone nuts.

"What's with *you*?" Shelby shot back.

Bettina kind of leaned close to me and whispered, "*I* think you're right, Cam."

This was actually very strange. I don't know if you have a big group of really close friends, but if you do, you know that really close friends don't go out of their way to say something supportive or nice. Like for instance if you and your friend are out surfing and you have a really awesome ride, your friend would say, "That all you got?" But if you saw some TV show about two friends, one of the TV friends might say, "You are the best surfer ever!" Real friends give each other a hard time all day long; then go home. So now, all of a sudden, Bettina started acting like a TV friend and said, "*I* think you're right, Cam." What was that about?

Luckily Mr. Mora was completely unaware of anything odd going on and said, "I agree this isn't about the treasure for Mr. Thorpe, but I'm not sure he financed this whole expedition just to satisfy his curiosity. One thing is certain: Mr. Thorpe has an agenda. We just don't know what that agenda is."

All of us were quiet for a moment. Maybe some of the Outriders were trying to figure out Mr. Thorpe's secret agenda. I know what I was thinking: *I'm hungry for pizza and my friends are acting weird.*

LANDING ON WATER

Everything about flying interested me: the way the propellers spun so fast that they looked like blurs in front of the engines, the way the plane bumped up and down on pockets of air, the way the horizon line disappeared when the pilot banked the aircraft to make a turn. I watched the wing flaps flutter up and down as the airplane descended through clouds. I had tried to push all the weirdness with the Outriders from my head and concentrate on the expedition ahead. It was almost sundown as we all looked out the bug's-eye windows of the PBY and got our first look at Willow Key.

My first thought was that we had taken a trip back in time—no people, no cars, no asphalt, no country clubs, no telephone poles, no mailboxes, in fact nothing except an infinite plain of short, scrubby mangrove trees and tall, pointy saw grass. The inland waterway that looped and twisted through the dark expanse was called Spider Bay. It was probably named that because the water looked like a web spread across the vast landscape. In the light of the setting sun, the water glowed silver, which contrasted with the inky blackness of the mangrove swamp and the last rosy glow of dusk that hung on the horizon.

I knew that Bobby was piloting the PBY to a place on the far edge of the wilderness preserve called Hammock Landing. Since we were arriving in the evening, Mr. Mora wanted us all to have a place to stay before we made camp in Willow Key. Apparently the only man-made structures in all of the wilderness preserve were in Hammock Landing. I could spot a few yellow lights in the distance ahead. The flaps of the flying boat angled upward and the PBY tilted toward earth. We had taken off from the Ellistown airport runway and were now planning to land on the waves of Spider Bay. I looked down at the small bump on my arm, a souvenir from my bee sting. Was it really only two days ago that I'd presided over the debacle that was the Mega-Wash? It seemed like years.

You might think that landing on water would be all smooth and gentle, but you would be wrong. From the moment the hull of the flying boat made contact with the water we started to bounce, like a rock skimming on top of the water of a pond. Maybe if we were in a seaplane that wasn't built during World War II more of the equipment would have stayed strapped to the floor, but as soon as we started bouncing, our backpacks and the buoyancy compensator vests started flying around the cabin. We were very lucky the air tanks stayed strapped down; otherwise a few of us could have been crushed. The only one who seemed unaffected by the flying scuba gear was Howie. Not much can annoy Howie once he is comfortable (which is most of the time). He was probably thinking about the huge bowl of kibble he consumed each and every day, much as I had been thinking about the pizza.

Finally the bouncing stopped and the seaplane's engines relaxed as Bobby angled the PBY toward a long weather-gray dock. An old, flickering neon sign announced that we had arrived at Rita Mae's Fish

Camp. About two dozen brightly colored power-boats with outboard motors were moored alongside the dock. The boats were older models, well cared for and bristling with fishing gear. I noticed that there were no cars anywhere in sight. I also noticed that there were no roads. It was like we had reached an outpost at the very edge of the world.

"No signal," Din said looking down at his cell phone that we liked to call "the Bahtphone." *Baht* is the Thai word for "shoe." One of Din and Nar's many cousins had sent the phone to the twins hidden in a Michael Jordan high-top. The phone always worked and no one received a bill. Beyond that, we never asked any questions.

"Mr. Thorpe lent us this," Mr. Mora said as he pulled out a much-larger-than-normal cell phone with a stubby six-inch antenna.

"Sattelite phone," Nar said as he examined the charcoal gray brick.

"In case of emergency," Mr. Mora said.

"We won't need it," Bettina said.

"What makes you say that?" Shelby said as she stood and stretched her legs.

"Mr. Mora's been here before," Bettina said as Bobby popped open the side door of the PBY and the wall of humidity hit us like a wet mop.

I consider myself pretty durable. I've been dragged over coral by riptides, broken two fingers playing basketball, and survived the massive poison sumac attack, but nothing in my life prepared me for the aggressive curtain of wetness that surrounded us in Willow Key. Sometimes it is humid in Surf Island. If it gets too bad all you have to do is take a walk to the beach and there is usually an ocean breeze that makes you feel better. But there was no ocean in Willow Key and no breeze. Picture being in a steamy hot shower with the shower curtain closed and never being able to get out.

I heard a woman's raspy voice say, "Y'all lube up?"

I looked down from the open door of the plane to find a fourteen foot Boston Whaler powerboat snugged up next to the PBY. The woman piloting the boat was small and thin with white-blond hair. I think she was in her thirties, but I'm really bad at guessing ages. She was wearing a uniform with dark green shorts and a lighter green shirt. On her shirt sleeve it said FISH AND GAME. A name tag on the front of the shirt read RITA MAE.

"I said, did y'all lube up?

"Huh?" was all I could think to say.

"For the skeeters. They'll eat you alive, pick your bones, and then start on your friends for dessert."

Mr. Mora held up a tube of insect repellent gel. "We're well supplied."

"Don't much matter how 'supplied' you are. You gotta lube it on like axle grease or you'll be snack food before I get you and all this gear to shore. I'm Rita Mae Thibodaux, by the way."

For some reason Mr. Mora had a kind of goofy smile when he said, "I'm Peter Mora, and these are my students."

"And what in God's name is *that*?" Rita Mae said, pointing at the 243-pound mastiff.

Nar said, "His name is Howie." Nar looked ready to pounce. He was fiercely protective of Howie and did not react well if Howie was insulted in any way.

"Thought y'all brought a water buffalo down to the Willow." Rita Mae smiled at Howie, who wagged his tail.

Nar took this as a good sign and relaxed. Rita Mae started helping a few of us into her boat and said, "Hope y'all are hungry."

No matter how much tension there was between certain members of the Outriders, we could all agree that we were hungry. It took about half an hour for

Rita Mae to ferry everyone from the flying boat to shore. We all took as much equipment as we could carry in the Boston Whaler.

I had never heard of a "fish camp" before. I know it sounds like some place that a large-mouth bass would spend the summer, but it turns out Rita Mae's was a normal bar and restaurant but could only be accessed by boat. The main building was made of the same weather-gray wood as the dock. The roof was slanted; the high side faced the water. Under the eaves there was a big deck with plastic tables and chairs overlooking the dock. The low side of the roof angled toward a row of small cabins. The cabins didn't have doors, just zippered mosquito nets, like the flaps of a tent. Inside the cabins there were hammocks instead of beds.

Rita Mae caught us staring at the accommodations. "Them hammocks keep you up above any pesky nutria."

"Nutria?" Din asked.

"Kind of a giant muskrat," Wyatt said.

"When you set up camp in the Willow, you keep your food away outta your tents—y'all hear me?" Rita Mae said pointing a finger at us.

"Yes, ma'am," Nar said.

Even though Rita Mae wasn't much taller than I

was, it seemed like she would be the wrong person to disobey.

I heard music coming from the bar. It seemed to be a live band. I also smelled the aroma of food. Fried food. I was ravenous.

"You're with fish and game *and* own this place?" Mr. Mora asked. His mouth was still bent up in a really dopey smile.

"And don't make a living at neither," Rita Mae said. "But business is looking up now that I got me a check for some boat rentals from Falcon's Lair Holdings, whatever the heck that is."

One of the conditions that Mr. Thorpe insisted on before he would fund the expedition to Willow Key was we never mention his name or our secret mission to dive the wreck of *L'Esperanza*. Obviously we could tell anyone we wanted about Mr. Mora's biomass study.

"That's the corporation funding our biomass study," Mr. Mora said. I think you should know that Mr. Mora is an ultra-honest guy. It would almost kill him not to tell the truth. Luckily everything he had just said about Falcon's Lair Holdings was true.

"Awful lot of scuba gear just to collect itty-bitty samples."

I could see Mr. Mora working very hard to think of something to say that wasn't a lie.

"That may be true," he said.

Rita Mae let the subject drop and headed for the restaurant. The whole hungry group of us followed.

"You kids find some open tables on the deck. I'll get you somethin' to eat and introduce you to your guide."

Mr. Mora looked surprised. "Guide?"

"You're not rentin' my boats and headin' off into the Willow without a guide."

"I've been down here a lot of times. I don't think a guide is necessary."

"I don't really pay much never mind to what you think. You got my boats, you got my guide."

At that moment a woman started singing. We had reached the deck of the fish camp and discovered a small stage at the far end of it. I was surprised to see that the "woman" singing was in fact a girl, older than I was, maybe fifteen, sixteen. (I told you I'm really bad at guessing ages.) A bunch of fisherman eating fried catfish were watching the girl sing. A trio of musicians (playing piano, bass, and fiddle) accompanied her.

The stage was really just a small platform with

enough room for the girl and the trio. There were no amplifiers or microphones; the girl was just facing the crowd and singing with nothing in front of her. There was one small spotlight that was focused on the singer and it made her white-blond hair kind of shine or glow against the dark backdrop of Spider Bay. I'm not a huge fan of country music. I hear it sometimes on the radio. Some songs are okay, some are kind of cheesy. But it wasn't the music that caught my attention here on the deck; it was the girl's voice. It was pure and clear one minute and kind of like a growl the next. I know only a few chords on guitar, so I'm not like a music expert or anything, but this girl sang way better than anyone I've heard live before.

The fiddle player kicked into high gear and the girl sang:

Don't ever pick a fight with a grizzly bear.
Don't you corner a badger, they don't fight fair.
Don't grab a cougar's tail and give it a whirl.
And don't you ever, ever lie to a country girl.
Because a country girl's heart is pure as gold.
She'll love you completely, till the world grows old.
But don't you let a country girl catch you lie.
You'll regret that day; it's the day that you'll die.

For some reason I wasn't hungry anymore, but really thirsty. My throat felt funny, like I couldn't swallow. Maybe it was from all the humidity.

"Who's *that*?" I asked Rita Mae.

"That there's your guide," Rita Mae said, "my daughter, Jolene."

"That's a cool name—Jolene," I said without taking my eyes off the stage.

"That's a cool name—Jolene," Bettina repeated in a sort of mocking tone.

I looked over to find her, Shelby, Ty, and the rest of the Outriders staring at me as if I had done something strange. All I had been doing was watching Jolene sing.

"What is the problem?"

"Nothing," Shelby said.

"Yeah really, nothing," Bettina said. For some unknown reason, both girls turned their backs on the stage and walked away from me to the other side of the deck.

Okay, now it was official. I realized a strange weirdness had crept into our lives, and if we didn't watch out, it would ruin the Outriders.

CHAPTER FIVE: FRACTURING

Twelve hours after the Outriders arrived at our base camp deep inside Willow Key, Petty Officer First Class Kevin Doherty of the United States Coast Guard arrived to administer emergency medical treatment. But I probably should tell you the stuff that happened before that or it will be hard to understand how Mr. Mora broke his ankle.

None of us got much sleep at Rita Mae's fish camp. Sure, it was hot and sticky and the mosquitoes were dive-bombing around the cabins. (The netting did next to nothing.) But most of us were just amped up to be on an expedition so far from Surf Island.

When you watch TV or movies, kids my age are always going off to Rome on a school trip, or traveling to the Greek Islands for a summer vacation. I don't think any one of us who grew up in the Flats had ever been to a hotel or even a *motel*. I know I haven't. So when a really rich guy from the Bluffs offers to let us take his *seaplane* to a place like Willow Key and dive a sunken wreck, I didn't want to miss a minute of it by *sleeping*.

All the guys were bunked in one cabin, the girls in the other. I made sure that my hammock was next to Ty's. I really wanted to have a few minutes alone with him to find out why he was acting so weirdly. I tried to think of just the best way to put it, but all I could come up with was, "Hey, what's up with you?"

Ty just swayed in his hammock and stared at the ceiling.

"Gonna be tough to ignore me for the rest of your life."

After a few more seconds of silence, Ty finally said, "Not ignoring. Thinking."

"About some stupid thing I did or said?"

"Not about you."

"You want to tell me what it *is* about?"

Ty said something in the Eastern European language that he speaks. Obviously I had no idea what he said, but I kind of got the hint the conversation was over.

In the dim glow of the moonlight I could see that Ty had taken his wallet out of his back pocket and was looking at something inside. I had no idea what was in the wallet, but Ty stared at it for a long time.

I'm not particularly good with long silences, so I said, "Well, good night."

Ty said something that sounded like "Laku nosh," then put his wallet away and closed his eyes.

See, again, if this had been a TV show or a movie, I would have known just the right thing to say to Ty and he would have told me everything he was thinking or feeling. But here in the real world, I felt just as confused *after* my talk with Ty as I did *before* it. Maybe Bettina could get Ty to tell her what was bothering him, but somehow I doubted it.

It was warm and humid all night, but when the sun came up in the morning it became *scorching* and humid. Also, it was NOISY. There was this kind of DRONING sound almost as loud as the engines of the PBY. It took me a few seconds to realize that BUGS were making all the noise—billions and billions of bugs. The air smelled of fried fish and die-sel fuel, but to me it was the aroma of adventure. I got my first good look at Hammock Landing in the daylight, and I noticed one thing right away: There was only ONE WILLOW TREE. This protected wilderness was called Willow Key and there was only *one* willow. I made a mental note to ask Mr. Mora about that.

"Let's saddle up ladies, and you other critters, too!" Rita Mae yelled from the dock as she began loading diving equipment into her Boston Whaler. Next to her Jolene was starting up the Evinrude outboard on an old Chris Craft Scorpion. It looked to be about a twenty footer. I hopped down into the powerboat to help her load our diving equipment (technically, Mr. Thorpe's equipment).

"You're a good singer," I said to Jolene.

"You got a name?"

"Oh, sorry. I'm Cam Walker."

"Don't you know, *Mr. Cam Walker*, you need to ask permission before hoppin' into someone's boat?"

"Oh. Right. Sorry again." I started to climb back out of the boat when I heard Jolene laughing.

"I'm just bustin' chops. What are *they* lookin' at?"

I turned and saw Shelby and Bettina standing near

their cabin looking back in my direction. I wasn't sure exactly what they were staring at, but they looked grumpy as if they hadn't slept well at all.

"What's their problem?" Jolene said.

"I don't know. They've been acting weird ever since we left."

"I don't know them girls, but I know that look. It's the same look I have when one of my boyfriends is talkin' up some new girl."

"Wha—? Wait. No, we're all, you know, friends. I mean, they're not . . . and I'm not . . . you know . . ."

Jolene laughed really hard. "I'm just bustin' chops, junior. Try to keep up or you'll get left behind."

Jolene picked up a tube of sunblock and tossed it to me.

"Put some on. You're red as a beet already."

About an hour later, all of us, including Mr. Mora and Howie, were loaded into the boats and under way. We were moving very slowly, not just because the boats were overloaded, but because, as Jolene explained, "Spider Bay is just a bunch of stumps, weeds, and sea cows hidin' under an inch of water."

"Sea cows?" Din asked.

"Manatees," Wyatt said before Jolene could reply, "the largest freshwater mammal."

"Boats are their biggest enemy," Mr. Mora added.

"Not a one of 'em don't have their backs all cut up by prop blades," Jolene said. "There oughtta be a law."

"There is." Mr. Mora looked kind of sad when he said it.

Far off in the distance I could see some sort of ultra-tall tower with a small shed sitting at the top. I noticed it because it was the only thing taller than the endless sea of mangrove bushes. It sort of looked like someone had jabbed the sharpened end of a pencil with a big stubby eraser into the line of the horizon.

"What's that thing?" I asked Jolene.

"US Forestry Service fire tower."

"Must be pretty scary climbing to that shed up there."

"Ranger by the name of Varsha Patel *lives in it*."

"Someone lives way up there?"

"Yep."

"Must be kind of lonely."

"Most park rangers like it that way. That big kid should apply for the job." Jolene motioned toward Ty. "Don't he say nothin'?"

Like I said, best friends can give each other a hard

time all day long, but people we just met didn't have that right.

"He only talks to people he trusts," I said.

"Don't get your boxers in a twist—he just looks kind of *sad* is all."

I looked toward the rear of the boat where Ty was sitting. Jolene was right. Ty wasn't happy. Even a stranger could see it.

My thoughts were interrupted by the crackle of Jolene's shortwave.

"We're putting in just beyond them cypress knees," Rita Mae radioed to her daughter.

As the Boston Whaler and the Chris Craft Scorpion rounded a bend of the inland waterway, we all got a first look at our campsite. An ancient wooden sign announced that we had arrived at Osprey Grove, which was nothing more than a bare patch of sandy ground about the size of a baseball diamond. In the center of the campsite, just about where the pitcher's mound would be, was a cement fire pit, which was the only man-made thing we had seen since leaving Hammock Landing. Osprey Grove would be our base camp for both Mr. Mora's biomass study and Mr. Thorpe's diving expedition.

A bunch of the other kids from our class *groaned* when they saw how "primitive" our campsite was. I suppose they were expecting hot showers and deluxe cabins or something. I just didn't understand their reaction. Didn't they realize this was a once-in-your-whole-lifetime-if-you-are-lucky opportunity? I looked over at my friends in the Outriders. I promise you I'm not saying that we are better or smarter than the other kids in our class (we are not)—but at least we all had the right attitude. We knew that we were going to have to dig holes with a shovel and make our own toilets—and we were amped up about it! So what if we wouldn't shower for five days? We had the rest of our lives to take showers! We were going to help our biology teacher with his research and dive the sunken wreck of a Spanish galleon. If you can't get amped up about something like that, you should just hang around in your den playing video games and never leave the house! I'm sorry I stopped telling you the story for a minute there, but sometimes the other kids in my class just *do not get it*.

It took only about a half hour to unload our gear from the two boats. We didn't bother bringing the diving gear ashore; we left it in Jolene's Scorpion.

The plan was for Rita Mae to return to Hammock landing in her Boston Whaler and for Jolene to stay with us so she could take us out to the wreck. Of course Jolene didn't know that we were planning on diving a sunken ship; she thought we had all the scuba gear to collect deep-water biomass samples. Or we hoped that was what she thought. Jolene seemed really smart, and under normal circumstances we wouldn't attempt to lie to her. But Mr. Thorpe had insisted we keep our expedition a secret and we intended to honor his request.

Jolene was watching us set up our tents when she said, "You spray the bottom of those?"

"Huh?" Din said.

"You spray them tents with Deet?"

"What?" Nar said.

"You gotta spray the bottom of those tents with bug repellent or y'all gonna have chiggers in your life, and trust me, you don't want them chiggers in your life."

"Are you trying to frighten us?" Shelby had her hands on her hips. I got the impression she did not like Jolene.

"No, little girl. I'm your *guide*. So I'm doin' my job and *guidin'* y'all."

That "little girl" comment did not go over well with Shelby.

"Well, it so happens, we have an actual *biology teacher* here with us. I think we'll let *him* tell us what to do, if you don't *mind*."

Mr. Mora was unpacking some of his scientific gear when he looked up and said, "All of you, spray insect repellent on the bottom of your tents! You don't want tiny parasites burrowing into your skin and causing infections!"

Jolene smiled in a kind of *told you* way. All the air seemed to deflate out of Shelby.

"Oh, whatever," she said, and began spraying bug spray on her tent.

"We'll make swamp rats of you kids yet!" Rita Mae yelled to us as she fired up her outboard and guided the Boston Whaler out into Spider Bay and away from our campsite.

While most of us were struggling to set up these eight-man North Face tents that Mr. Thorpe had lent us, Mr. Mora was wasting no time setting up his equipment. He had assembled this thing he called a Fisher Scientific Balance. It kind of looked like an electronic scale you would weigh cold cuts on at the deli section of a supermarket. It had a stainless steel plate floating over a square metal box with a digital readout. But instead of weighing stuff like half pounds of roast beef, the Fisher Scientific Balance weighed stuff in really TINY amounts called "micrograms." The scale was so sensitive that Mr. Mora had to put up a wind screen around the device so that even a small breeze did not throw off the measurements.

We all became kind of mesmerized watching Mr. Mora work. Most of us left the North Face tents half-assembled, and gathered around our biology teacher to watch him set up his experiment. I know it might not sound incredibly interesting watching a guy zero-out a scientific balance, but Mr. Mora is so into biology, his enthusiasm kind of rubs off on everyone around him. Even the kids who had complained about the Osprey Grove campsite were now helping Mr. Mora unpack duffle bags of beakers and filters. You could have shot a bazooka right over Mr. Mora's head and I don't think he would have noticed; that's how charged up he was about his work.

"Let's take a test sample. See if all the equipment is working," Mr. Mora said. He held out a glass beaker. "Bettina, why don't you collect our first sample of periphyton."

Bettina took the beaker but didn't move. She had no idea what Mr. Mora had asked her to do, and none of the rest of us did either. Of course Mr. Mora knew this would be the case, and he smiled.

"Okay, time for a little science."

BIOLOGY 101

Look, like I said, I'm not Mr. Biology. So I'll just tell you the things you need to know about Mr. Mora's biomass experiment, because it has a lot to do with what happened in Willow Key and all the people who wanted to make sure we never left.

Actually the experiment wasn't that hard to understand. Even *I* could wrap my brain around it. Basically it came down to measuring how much living stuff (plants and animals) were in a sample of water. Periphyton is just a technical name for the mucky stuff you find in swamps. Mr. Mora had Bettina scoop up a beaker full of gunk from the shoreline. Then he carefully sucked the gunk into a long glass straw that he called a "pipette." This was so that he could measure out an exact amount of periphyton. Then he took a piece of filter paper, which looked a lot like a coffee filter your parents would use in a home coffee machine, and put it under the pipette.

Then Mr. Mora let the all the periphyton drip onto the filter. All the gunky stuff that was in the water stayed on top of the filter in a little green clump. Then Mr. Mora weighed the filter and the clump on the Fisher Scientific Balance.

Since Mr. Mora had been down to Willow Key many times before, he had taken a lot of these biomass measurements. By comparing earlier samples to newer samples he could figure out if there was MORE plant and animal life or LESS. Mr. Mora was convinced there was LESS periphyton than in previous years, which meant that Willow Key was slowly DYING. Mr. Mora thought he even knew WHY the periphyton was being killed off: mercury. Mercury is real helpful in a thermometer but it is really, really poisonous for plants and animals.

Mr. Mora explained that there were two ways to test for mercury. There was the complicated scientific way in a lab using an ultra-expensive machine called a "mass spectrometer," but the nearest one of those was hundreds of miles from Willow Key. Mr. Mora was using a "field test" for mercury. This didn't measure the *amount* of mercury, it just detected if there was any mercury in the periphyton. The field test for mercury was the one part of the biomass experiment that Mr. Mora wouldn't let any of us help with because it involved some nasty chemicals. According to a worksheet Mr. Mora handed out, for the mercury field test you need:

1. Pure water
2. Nitrogen gas
3. Bromine monochloride (BrCl) (dangerous)
4. Hydrochloric acid (HCl) (super-dangerous)

Mr. Mora put all the chemical stuff in a cylindrical beaker with the periphyton. Then he stretched a clear balloon filled with nitrogen gas across the top of the beaker. We all watched as the clear balloon turned ORANGE.

A few of us said, "OOOOH," like Mr. Mora had done some type of magic trick.

"That orange color in the balloon means there is mercury in Spider Bay."

Then we all felt kind of foolish for *oooh*ing.

Shelby raised her hand. Even though we were in the middle of a vast wilderness, old habits die hard. Mr. Mora nodded toward her.

"I don't get one thing. If you know there is less biomass here in Willow Key, and you know the mercury is causing it, why are we even here? You already have solved the big question."

"I haven't even come close to solving the big question."

"But you discovered the mercury!" Din said.

"But *where* is the mercury coming from?" Mr. Mora asked. "There isn't any heavy industry near Willow Key. So why is there mercury in the water? Until I solve *that* mystery, my research means very little."

"But you'll figure it out, right?" Wyatt said.

"I hope so."

Bettina said, "But even if you don't figure it out, you'll still get your PhD?"

"It's my job to worry about you guys, not the other way around."

Mr. Mora had said the same thing after the disaster of the Mega-Wash. This time it made me feel even sadder.

"We'll help you figure it out," Wyatt said.

I tried to smile and nod in agreement, but I felt like a phony. How were a bunch of middle school biology students supposed to unlock a huge chemical/biological mystery that our own teacher couldn't figure out?

I didn't have much time to ponder the issue because at that moment, Ty started yelling.

TY'S WALLET

You have to understand, I've never heard Ty yell. Not even once. I play on the basketball team with Ty, and we've been in some really close games (regional quarterfinals), and he hasn't even yelled when he's been called for a really ticky-tack foul that cost us a game. But now Ty was yelling stuff in his own language and looking all over the campsite for something.

"What's up with the sad kid?" Jolene asked me.

"I have no idea," I said as I rushed to Ty's side.

"Wallet gone!" Ty yelled as he frantically pushed aside each and every tent searching for it.

"Ty, relax. Maybe it's in your backpack," Shelby said as she rushed over to her friend.

"Not in backpack!" Ty almost looked like he might cry.

"We should check the boat," Nar said. He brought Howie with him on the premise that the mastiff would be able to sniff out the missing wallet.

Jolene followed after Nar and the 243-pound dog; they all climbed into the Chris Craft.

Ty was now about to push aside the scientific equipment. Mr. Mora put a hand on his shoulder, as if to calm Ty down. This had the opposite effect and Ty got even more upset.

"Wallet gone!"

Mr. Mora spoke very calmly and evenly. "Ty, I know you're very upset. We'll look everywhere for the wallet. Are you worried about the money? Because I can—"

Ty didn't let Mr. Mora finish. "Not money!" Ty was charging around like some kind of wild dog, frantically looking everywhere.

Bettina stepped in front of him. "Ty, we're not going to leave this campsite until we find your wallet. Calm down and let's retrace your steps."

Somehow Bettina had managed to get through to Ty. He looked down as if ashamed.

"Must to find."

"We will," Bettina said.

"Let's all fan out and search in a grid pattern!" Mr. Mora said as if he was the commander of a military unit.

None of us understood why Ty had gone so crazy, but we all understood that finding the wallet was CRUCIAL. We had all known Ty since fourth grade, and he had never acted this way even ONCE.

So we fanned out. We all started marching back and forth as if we were mowing a lawn, being careful to search every inch of Osprey Grove. Mr. Mora had taken a grid on the perimeter near a row of cypress trees.

"OW!" I heard him say.

I looked over toward Mr. Mora and saw him peering down at the ground. Had he found the wallet?

"OWWWWWWW!" He screamed. Everyone, even Ty, raced over to our biology teacher.

"What kind of ants are those?" Shelby said pointing to one of Mr. Mora's shoes, which was covered with THOUSANDS of tiny red ants.

"FIRE ANTS!" Wyatt yelled.

"OWWWWWWWWWWWWWW!" Mr. Mora screamed as he started hopping around as if his leg were boiling in oil. About a millisecond later we all heard a loud *SNAP* like the sound a tree branch makes when you run over it with your bicycle. Only this wasn't a branch, It was Mr. Mora's ankle.

For some strange reason Jolene pushed her way through the crowd of students and dumped a gerry can of GASOLINE onto Mr. Mora's broken foot.

"WHAT ARE YOU DOING?" Shelby said to Jolene.

"Killin' them fire ants!"

"Din, get that Sat phone," I said. Then I turned to Jolene. "Who do we call?"

"Way out here? The Coasties."

Three and a half hours later, Petty Officer First Class Kevin Doherty climbed out of his Coast Guard motor lifeboat and carried his bright red medical emergency kit toward the campsite.

He looked around to find:

1. Twenty middle school students
2. A sixteen-year-old river guide
3. A biology teacher with a badly swollen ankle writhing in pain on top of a flattened North Face eight-man tent

Petty Officer First Class Doherty stopped for a moment as if catching wind of something.

"I smell gasoline," he said.

"To kill the fire ants," I said.

Petty Officer First Class Doherty looked down. Not only was Mr. Mora's ankle swollen to the size of a grapefruit, it looked as if had been chewed on by piranhas.

Petty Officer Doherty shook his head and sighed. He knelt down and clicked open his emergency medical kit, which looked like an enormous fishing tackle box. He didn't look at any of us as he took out his first-aid supplies.

"I'm going to splint and bandage up your teacher here. Give him an injection to take down the swelling. Then I need you all to do something very important. . . ."

We all leaned closer to hear what Petty Officer First Class Doherty had to say.

"I want you all to GO HOME."

CHAPTER SIX: TREASURING

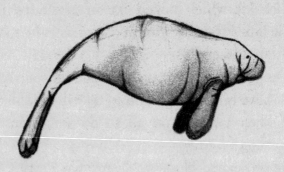

"**N**o," I said.

"Come again, son?" Petty Officer First Class Kevin Doherty of the United States Coast Guard was used to having people obey his orders. He was extremely tall, over six feet five (I am very good at judging heights, I play basketball), and it looked like you could land an airplane on his shoulders.

"We're not going home," I said. I folded my arms across my chest as if to emphasize my point. My eyes were dead level with Petty Officer Doherty's shirt pocket. I couldn't help noticing that he had won a medal for sharpshooting.

All of my friends, Mr. Mora, and Jolene Thibodaux watched the confrontation, their heads pivoting back and forth like they were at a tennis match.

"Your teacher fractured his ankle."

"I know that, sir. He broke it helping my friend find his wallet." I looked over at Ty. I could tell he was feeling responsible for what had happened and it hadn't helped at all that I had brought it up with Petty Officer Doherty. I make mistakes like this all the time.

Mr. Mora looked over at the pair of aluminum crutches the Coast Guard officer had put beside him. "Cam, we're going to do what Petty Officer Doherty tells us to do."

"I'm sorry, but we're not, Mr. Mora. If we leave now you can't finish your research."

"It doesn't matter."

"But it does!" I turned to Petty Officer Doherty. "A doctor is just going to put a cast on Mr. Mora's ankle and tell him to rest up, right?"

"The key word there is *doctor*."

"I know. But you did a great job with that splint. If Mr. Mora keeps off his feet and keeps the ankle elevated, three or four days won't make a difference, will it?"

Petty Officer Doherty's radio crackled. He moved a distance away to listen to the transmission from base. I have no idea what was said to him, but he replied, "Copy that. Over."

Petty Officer Doherty walked back toward us. "We've got a cargo vessel that strayed out of the shipping lanes and ran aground. They were operating where they shouldn't have been—just like you people. I can't force you to leave, but I strongly urge you to abandon this campsite. The Willow sounds like an inviting place, but I can assure you that it is not." Then to Mr. Mora he said, "Sir, is there anything further you need?"

"Some better luck would help," Mr. Mora said.

"My commanding officer says that we all make our own luck. I'll leave you with that piece of advice." Petty Officer First Class Doherty strode back toward his motor lifeboat and powered off toward his next rescue mission.

Jolene was the first to speak. "I'm thinkin' I should radio my mama and get her back here."

"No! We didn't come all this way to give up," I said. "Mr. Mora, do you think you can make it for a few more days?"

"Yes, but—"

I didn't let my teacher finish. "We'll split up into two groups. Jolene will take Shelby, Bettina, Ty, Wyatt, and me to dive the . . . bay for deeper bio-mass samples."

Din and Nar looked at me and both said, "Hey!"

"Nar, there's no shade on the boat. We can't leave Howie baking in the sun. And Din, you're the Sat phone guy; we need you here with Mr. Mora and the rest of the class in case you have to call in help. Also you guys can use Howie and keep looking for Ty's wallet."

For the moment this seemed to satisfy Din and Nar. They, like the rest of us, hated to be left out of any cool expedition. If this were a normal situation I would have suggested we all dive the wreck of *L'Esperanza*, but circumstances had stopped being normal ever since the Mega-Wash. Leaving Howie out in the sun without shade was only one huge problem. The other was the fact that Din and Nar had almost no experience diving. They could snorkel as well as anyone, but just didn't have enough hours with a scuba tank. So many things had gone wrong already; I just couldn't risk one more bad thing happening.

"Cam, I appreciate what you are trying to do,

but I can't agree to it," Mr. Mora said.

"Mr. Mora, hardly anything's changed. You were going to be at base camp taking periphyton levels. The rest of us were going to be collecting samples. The only thing different is that you're going to be doing it lying down or on crutches."

Mr. Mora thought about this for a moment. I knew what I said made sense. I really wanted to come through for Mr. Mora. But I also knew that, deep down, part of the reason I was fighting so hard to stay was because I just *had to* dive the wreck and be a part of Mr. Thorpe's treasure hunt. Sometimes when I take a good long look inside myself, I'm not that proud of what I see.

"I'll tell you what, Cam—I really want to get those deep-water samples. Why don't the group of you go do the dive, and when you come back we'll see how things are going?"

Here's the thing about adults: They are smart. So many kids make the mistake of forgetting that one simple concept. Mr. Mora must have had some kind of window into my brain. He knew how much I wanted to dive the Spanish galleon. To the rest of the group I may have looked like the guy who was helping out our biology teacher, but only Mr. Mora and I would know the truth: I was the one being helped.

L'ESPERANZA

Just as Shelby, Bettina, Wyatt, Ty, and I were about to board Jolene's Chris Craft Scorpion, Mr. Mora called to me. "Cam!"

I turned and Mr. Mora was holding up Nalgene plastic sample collection bottles. "Don't you need these?"

I had been so amped up to dive the wreck, I had *completely forgotten* our "cover story" about collecting deep-water biomass samples.

I walked back to Mr. Mora and took the bottles. He whispered to me, "Don't forget to actually take some samples."

"I get it. To keep up appearances."

"No, I would really like to see the samples, to see how far the mercury has spread."

"So, you mean the dive could actually help your research?"

"I think it might."

As I walked back toward Jolene's boat, I was feeling much better. By diving the wreck, we were also helping our biology teacher. It was kind of a win-win situation. At least that was what I told myself as I got on the boat, and Jolene nudged the throttle and we slowly made our way along the twisting inland waterway toward the spot where Spider Bay met the sea.

When we were a few hundred yards from shore, Jolene killed the engine. She then took the key out of the ignition. We drifted for a few moments. Wyatt looked down at a portable GPS device that Mr. Thorpe had leant us. "We're nowhere near the dive site," he said.

"What's going on?" Bettina said to Jolene.

"That's what I wanna know," Jolene said. "The bunch of you ain't divin' for no *samples*."

"Yes, we are." I held up the Nalgene containers that Mr. Mora had given me.

"Y'all don't need scuba gear to dive for samples. A snorkel and flippers would be easier and faster. The spot where y'all want to dive is right over an old shipwreck. And"—Jolene looked right at me—"*that* fool clean forgot to take the sample bottles!" Jolene put her hands on her hips and glared at us. "I may be a swamp rat, but I'm not stupid!"

I couldn't blame Jolene for being angry. We were lying to her (or at least concealing the truth) and she knew it. We had been thrown a curve; we never expected to have a guide along with us. Mr. Thorpe had asked us to keep the mission a secret, but he assumed we would be piloting our own rented boat. We were in a tough situation and I didn't know what to do.

"This here's my boat, or at least it's my mama's. How do I know y'all aren't up to something illegal? Or dangerous? I'm not starting up this outboard unless I get some answers."

Shelby, Bettina, Wyatt, and Ty looked right at me. I guess they were expecting me to figure a way out of this problem. Like I said, and this isn't bragging, I'm kind of the guy who makes the plans. But a lot of things I had arranged for the Expedition to Willow Key had imploded, and I wasn't feeling my most confident. As I saw it, there were only two choices:

1. Think of an air-tight lie.
2. Tell the truth.

Technically, there was a third choice of tossing Jolene overboard and pirating her boat, but that was more of what one of the ultra-bad guys in a Tom Cruise movie would do, so it wasn't a realistic option.

"We're going to dive the wreck of *L'Esperanza*

and try to find a clue to a long-lost treasure."

"Yeah, right," Jolene said.

"I don't blame you for not believing me, but that's what we're doing."

Shelby tapped me on the shoulder. "Why'd you do that?"

"Think about it. It's Jolene's boat—if we don't tell her the truth, we don't get to dive the wreck. And I think we can trust her."

"Oh, I bet you do," Shelby said.

"What's that supposed to mean?"

"Oh, like you don't know we know," Bettina said.

I was more confused than ever.

Wyatt started to speak. "But Mr.—"

I quickly clamped my hand over Wyatt's mouth. I had made the decision to reveal our mission, but not the person who sent us. I could at least honor Mr. Thorpe's request that far. Wyatt pulled my hand away from his face. He was angry.

"What's up with *that*?"

"Stop!"

We all looked over at Ty. This was the first word he had spoken in some time.

"We not fight!" He looked right at Jolene. "Must to go."

Even Jolene knew to listen to Ty when he was this upset. She just shook her head as if to say, *What a bunch of idiots*. She turned the key in the ignition and pushed the throttle forward.

I made my way to the cockpit of the boat.

"Sorry about that. We all thought it would be better to keep what we were doing a secret."

As she used the compass to point the boat on the proper heading, she said to me, "Why would I care if you dive that wreck? It's been picked over by every diver that ever came to the Willow. There's nothin' for you to find."

"You're probably right. But we dug up some new information. It probably doesn't mean anything."

"But *you* think it does."

"*L'Esperanza*."

"Isn't that the name of the sunken ship?"

"It means '*The Hope*.'"

Jolene smiled. "You're a weird one, junior," she said, then tousled my hair, kind of like how someone would pet their Labrador.

When I looked around at Bettina and Shelby, they were glowering at me. Shelby tossed a tube of sunscreen in my direction.

"You need to reapply."

CARRIED AWAY

About three hours later Wyatt heard a beep from the GPS device. "We're here!" he said.

Jolene threw the anchor overboard. "That anchor chain there is your point of reference. Y'all keep that in sight and know where it is at all times. There's tricky currents all over this bay."

It took about a half hour for all of us to gear up for the dive. None of us said very much—we were mainly checking and rechecking the equipment. Wyatt considered himself the "dive master" and was very exact about all of us following procedure. He was the only one of us who had actually become junior certified. His parents had insisted on it. Navy people do things a certain way.

Mr. Thorpe had lent us the best equipment known to man: Sherwood aluminum compressed air tanks and Suunto depth gauges. I couldn't imagine ever having this type of gear on my back ever again. When we were all geared up and ready for the dive, I reached into my backpack and pulled out a water-proof pouch. Inside were our instructions from Mr. Thorpe. Our benefactor had asked me to not open the dive instructions until we were out on the boat ready to enter the water. He only wanted the Out-riders to know about the search for the treasure. He had told me it was because "we could be trusted." If only Mr. Thorpe knew we had already violated his trust by telling Jolene about our expedition.

I opened the plastic pouch. Shelby, Bettina, Wyatt, and Ty crowded around me in a tight circle. Jolene walked back from the cockpit; she, too, wanted to see what we were looking at.

I pulled out three waterproof laminated sheets of paper.

1. A SCHEMATIC DIAGRAM OF *L'ESPE-RANZA*: This drawing of the sunken Spanish galleon showed how the ship was situated on the bottom of Spider Bay. The ship had come to rest on a steep incline. The bow (front) of the ship was on the low side of the incline, pointing toward the sea floor. The stern (rear) of the boat was on the high side of the incline closest to the surface. The diagram had a big red circle around TWO UPRIGHT WOODEN POSTS on the deck of the stern. None of us knew what this meant. Yet.

2. A COPY OF THE ACTUAL SHIP'S LOG: This was written in Spanish (duh) and with very old-fashioned penmanship. There was another red circle around a passage of text and below it was the translation in English:

Dearest Dona Juliana,

If you find this ship's log, I am gone.

But my sword remains where I left it—in the column.

It points the way back to your treasure.

Your family's riches allowed my escape.

My escape cost me our love.

Forgive me, dearest.

3. OUR DIVE INSTRUCTIONS FROM MR. THORPE: These were actually very short and simple. A typed note read:

Dear Outriders,

You will notice that there is a red circle on the diagram of *L'Esperanza*. On the rear deck of the ship there are two columns that adorned the entrance to the captain's quarters. I believe that in one of these columns is hidden the sword El Trueno speaks of in the ship's log. The sword might be in the form of a real weapon, it might be a drawing or diagram, or you might look for the word *spada*, which is the Spanish word for "sword." I have lent you a video camera with an underwater housing so that you may photograph the expedition. If you find a clue that cannot be salvaged, you can make a video to bring back with you. Below find diagrams of Spanish swords of the era. Best of luck with the expedition.

The diving instructions were not signed. There were eight examples of different Spanish swords at the bottom of the laminated sheet. It was a long, tough road to get to this point, but now that we were here, I couldn't think of anything cooler I could be doing.

I looked up to find Jolene with an odd look on her face. I think she'd finally realized we weren't just some dumb kids who watched too many shows on the Discovery Channel.

"Who gave you all that stuff?" Jolene asked.

"I'm not allowed to tell you," I said. "But now you know exactly what we're going to be doing down there. That will have to be enough."

"I'm cool," Jolene said. But the tone of her voice had changed. She had stopped speaking to me as if I was some little boy. It made me feel kind of good and sort of thirsty. I don't know why.

About a minute later Wyatt, who was holding the

underwater video rig, demonstrated the proper way to fall backward off of a boat while wearing scuba gear. Within seconds, all of the rest of us had followed him into the water.

Mr. Thorpe's diagram of *L'Esperana* did not prepare me for what we would see once we were underwater.

Just like in the diagram, the shipwreck was on an incline, but that very steep slope was A CORAL REEF. The reef was EXPLODING with color. There are tiny patches of coral near Surf Island, and even a few small reefs, but this CITY OF CORAL stretched for hundreds of yards in every direction. The reef was terraced and angled sharply downward, like the steps of a football stadium. The wreck of *L'Esperanza* had become *part of the reef.* Over the years the coral had grown up, around, and through the vessel, as if the ship had always been a natural part of the reef. Miraculously the original wooden timbers of the ship had endured and had become home to anemones, sponges, clown fish, trigger fish, sea stars, spiny lobsters, wolf eels, barracuda, nudibranches, crabs, sea urchins, sea cucumbers, coral shrimp, angelfish, sand sharks, sea horses, bat rays, and guitarfish.

I was sorry Mr. Mora wasn't around to see the reef. It was as if the pages of the biology textbook we read in his class had come to life and surrounded us. Shelby, Bettina, Wyatt, and Ty were all staring in amazement at the seascape below us. Wyatt took some video images of the reef and the wreck. He then (in his role as dive master) gave us a hand signal to begin our descent.

The stern of *L'Esperanza* was only about fifteen feet below our position. This was to be the moment of truth. We had come all this way, and finally we would be reaching back three hundred years for a clue to a buried pirate treasure. The diagram Mr. Thorpe had provided was extremely accurate. It took only a few seconds for us to find the two upright wooden posts that were in fact mahogany columns that had been decorated with a swirl pattern, like the way soft ice cream looks when it goes into a cone. Wyatt hovered about five feet above us, videoing every angle of the ship and particularly the columns. Shelby and Bettina examined the column to the left. Ty and I looked over the column on the right.

Mr. Thorpe had provided us with underwater flashlights. We all clicked them on even though it was extremely bright at the stern. There were dark shadows cast by some of the overhanging woodwork of the ship and we didn't want to take any chances on missing the clue left by El Trueno.

Ty and I were very methodical. We started at the base of the right column and looked at every inch of it all the way to the top. We then ran our fingers along the swirls of wood. Next we tried to push on the mahogany to see if there were any hidden compartments. We looked for carvings, symbols, messages—anything that might contain the image of a sword. No matter how hard we looked, there was nothing there.

When I turned toward Shelby and Bettina, they were both giving me the thumbs-down. By this time Wyatt had moved in for close-ups of the columns. He had a powerful underwater strobe light trained on the wooden posts and was carefully recording every square inch of the doorway to the captain's quarters. After he finished, he shook his head as if to say, *I didn't find anything either.*

Finally Wyatt gave us the hand signal to surface, and we all slowly rose into the bright sunlight. The moment our scuba masks broke the surface, everyone took out their mouthpieces and began talking at once.

"Maybe someone found it before we did," Bettina said.

"Maybe the sword is hidden *inside* the columns," I said.

"I tapped on them. They're solid wood," Wyatt said.

"Is no sword," Ty said, and that ended the discussion for the moment.

"How'd you guys do?" Jolene called from the boat.

"Not so good," I said as I climbed back on board.

"Maybe El Trueno was lying," Bettina said.

Shelby, who hadn't said much, picked up one of the laminated sheets. "I don't think he was lying," she said. "Listen to this." Shelby read from the captain's log. "'Your family's riches allowed my escape. My escape cost me our love. Forgive me dearest.' Why would he write that if it weren't true?"

"I don't know, maybe because he was a *pirate*," Wyatt said.

Shelby grunted like she was frustrated we all weren't getting her point. She did this a lot, as her brain worked more quickly than the rest of ours. "If El Trueno didn't really love Dona Juliana, he would never have written the note. I think he felt horrible about what he had done. He had to escape from

Sternmetz and the only way for him to do it was to steal money from the woman he loved. All he could hope for was that Dona Juliana would somehow get his note and know that he truly loved her. There was no Internet three hundred years ago."

"You get all of that from one little note?" I said.

Shelby shot me a look. "It's so clear. Even in the Spanish, you can see that . . . wait a minute."

Shelby examined the laminated sheet more closely. Then she picked up the diagram of the sunken ship and stared at that for a few seconds. "We have to go back down! I think I know where the sword is!"

We all crowded around Shelby. She pointed at the original document from El Trueno's captain's log. "It's the translation! It's wrong! I mean, it's right, but it's wrong!"

"Okay, I'm lost," I said.

"See this word in the Spanish—*columna*? It means 'column,' but it also means 'spine.' Most people say *spina*, but you can also say *columna*!"

"So?" Bettina said.

"*So*, there's one of those mermaids on the front of the boat!" Shelby pointed toward the diagram of *L'Esperanza* and pointed to the carving of a woman on the bow.

"It's called a figurehead," Wyatt said.

"Whatever. But the figurehead is of a *woman*!"

"But the word *spine* could refer to anything!" I said.

Shelby grunted again. Our brains were lagging behind hers and she was frustrated. "Don't you see? It's all in what El Trueno wrote! 'The sword remains where I left it, in the *spine*!' It is a fancy way to say, 'I stabbed you in the back!' I bet you if we go back down there and look at that figurehead, we're going to find the sword!"

"It makes sense," Jolene said. "Maybe it was something the pirate thought that only the woman would understand. Like if you text message something to your boyfriend that only he gets and no one else."

I said to Wyatt, "How are we doing with compressed air?"

"We've all got extra tanks."

"Then what do we have to lose?" I said.

Shelby smiled. So did everyone else. I even caught Jolene smiling. She was now totally into the treasure hunt. I knew I was right to have trusted her.

Wyatt got busy connecting our backup tanks. As he worked, the dive master issued instructions: "The figurehead is much deeper. I'd say about forty-four feet. That means we'll be past one atmosphere of pressure. We can only stay down a really short time if we don't want to do a decompression dive."

"How much time do we have?" I asked.

"Let's say fifteen minutes to be safe. Stay with me," Wyatt said. Somehow, once he had appointed himself dive master, Wyatt had transformed into a Navy SEAL.

Once we were back in the water, Wyatt had us hang at about ten feet to do an air and buoyancy check. Suddenly a dark shadow moved across us. Something large was blocking us from the sun, and it was *moving*. My first thought was *SHARK*, and I looked up. What I saw will stay with me always. The animal moving above us was a lot larger than a shark. At least it was a lot heavier. It was a MANA-TEE. And it was staring down at us, curious what was causing all the bubbles.

I knew that it was a manatee because Mr. Mora had shown us a film about the largest freshwater mammals. They weigh up to a ton and have whiskers kind of like a walrus, but no tusks. In fact, a manatee kind of looks like a tuskless walrus smashed together with the tail of a two thousand pound beaver.

Even though it was one of the coolest things any of us would ever see, we had a mission to accomplish and very little time. Wyatt led the way with the video camera and we all stayed very close to the dive master. Once we got midway down the length of the ship, I noticed something really dramatic happening with the reef. Up above, the reef was bursting with life, but down here the coral seemed to be dying and there were almost no fish or plants swaying in the currents.

Bettina tapped me on the shoulder and pointed to our right. I saw something very odd. It was an old cement pipe, completely encrusted with barnacles. The pipe seemed to angle toward shore. It was almost impossible to see, it blended in so well with its surroundings, but the mouth of the pipe was perfectly round and it stuck out as man-made even down here in the depths. Bettina and I trained our flashlights on the open end of the pipe and we could see yellowish-brown liquid gushing out into the bay. What was up with that?

I felt Bettina taking one of the Nalgene bottles that I had attached to my buoyancy regulator vest. I had completely forgotten to take a sample for Mr. Mora during the first dive. Treasure hunting had made me completely lose my mind. Luckily Bettina kept her head and scooped up a sample of the yellowish-brown gunk coming from the pipe.

I hovered above Bettina for a moment, and then when she was finished screwing the top on the sample bottle, we both rejoined the group near the bow of the boat. It was much darker down there than it had been at the stern. We were relying a lot on our underwater flashlights to see. The whole scene was kind of eerie. We were surrounded by a forest of dead coral and staring up at the carved wooden image of a woman that jutted out from the prow of the boat.

The figurehead was in amazingly good shape. It depicted a young woman with long flowing hair. Her arms were at her sides but slightly extended away from her body as if she were trying to float on the wind. I don't think they surfed back in the days of El Trueno, but the figurehead reminded me of a woman trying to keep her balance on a longboard. In the beam of my flashlight, I could still see flecks of gold paint on the woman's hair and chips of red paint on her dress. I couldn't believe that those small bits of color had survived all these years.

Shelby was not wasting any time. She was examining the ornately carved area where the back of the figurehead (the spine) was attached to the ship.

The wood in this area was carved with all types of knobby bumps and scrolls. (I don't know much about old wood carvings.)

I saw Wyatt glancing at his dive watch. He was concerned about how long we had been at this depth. Suddenly I heard a gurgle, like Shelby had lost her air hose or something.

I looked over and saw that Shelby wasn't struggling to breathe, she was trying to *shout*. She was jiggling some of the carved knobby wood, and a section of it had *pulled away*. We all crowded around because that knobby piece of wood had turned out to be THE HILT of a sword, and as Shelby was sliding it away from the boat, we saw THE SWORD'S BLADE glinting in our flashlights!

Shelby had been right! El Trueno's sword had been hidden in plain sight, right at the prow of his ship. Shelby tugged on the hilt and the sword came free. It wasn't shiny stainless steel, but a dull brown, as you would expect from spending three hundred years in salt water. But the strangest thing about the sword was that there were THREE SMALL HOLES about eight inches apart on the blade. The holes weren't round; they were diamond-shaped.

Shelby handed me the sword and I took a close look

at it. I had no clue why there were three diamond-shaped holes punched into the blade, but I did know one thing: I would have no time to figure it out because all five of us were swept away by a surge of water so powerful that it almost sucked the scuba mask off my face.

CHAPTER SEVEN: SURFACING

As a surfer, I get caught in dangerous currents all the time. The worst is the riptide. A riptide can not only ruin your day, it can destroy your life. You can be pulled out to sea, you can be sucked under the surf, and worst of all—you can lose all your strength trying to fight it.

But Shelby, Bettina, Wyatt, Ty, and I weren't caught in a riptide. It was something else, something I hadn't really experienced before. This was more of a SURGE, like you would see near a tide pool. We were all being SUCKED away from the reef. I knew my friends were all experienced ocean swimmers and wouldn't panic in a strong current. They all knew to just let the ocean do its thing and ride out the flow. But this wasn't just a random ocean current. We had a very good reason to panic: We were being sucked into a dark underwater CAVE.

Actually, it was more of an underwater *gap in the rocks*. There was a very good chance we would never make it through the gap; we would just be thrashed against the jagged edges of the rocks.

The surge had pushed the five of us very close together. For some reason I was at the leading edge of the group. We were about fifteen yards from the gap in the rocks, which from our angle looked like the jaws of an enormous great white shark. I realized I was still clutching El Trueno's sword. As kind of a last-ditch attempt to save our lives, just as we were being sucked into the black hole, I jammed the blade into the overhanging edge of the gap. This created a kind of chain reaction. Somehow the blade buried deep into a crevice between some boulders. This slowed my momentum and caused Shelby, Bettina, Wyatt, and Ty to smash into my back. The five of us formed a large clump. Ty spread his long, powerful arms and pulled us all into a huddle. The surge of water rushed all around us, but we were like a bottle stopper that was too big for the bottle. Together, in a clump, we were too large to be sucked into the abyss. If the surge had lasted for a few seconds longer, we wouldn't have been able to stay together. But, with the same speed that it appeared, the surge ended.

We didn't hesitate for even one second. I pulled El Trueno's sword from between the boulders and joined the rest of the group shooting up toward the surface. Proper dive technique would have been to take our time, but we weren't thinking about the dive manual. We were thinking about getting to the surface and away from the horrifying dark gap in the rocks.

I popped my head out of the water, ripped off my mask, and took a big inhale of air. I had plenty of compressed air left in my tank, but I needed real out-in-the-sunshine air to realize I was still alive. All of my friends did the exact same thing. I watched them each take a big inhale of noncompressed air and smile at the joy of being safe.

I realized two things about our current position.

1. The good thing: We were only about forty yards from shore.
2. The bad thing: I had no idea where we were and could not see Jolene or her boat.

The only logical thing for us to do was to swim to shore. You have never seen a group of five people wearing heavy scuba gear get out of the water faster. We unzipped our vests, threw off our flippers, and fell back onto a small spit of sand. I staked El Trueno's sword in the earth and claimed this tiny beach for the Outriders.

"Problem." Apparently dive master Wyatt was not taking the time to savor our escape from death.

"What's the problem, Wyatt?" Shelby said.

"Aside from the obvious," I said.

"We have no com." This was Wyatt-speak for "communications."

"Okay," I said.

"There's no way for us to contact Jolene. That riptide, or whatever it was, might have dragged us miles away. Once Jolene catches on that we're missing, how's she going to find us? There's like a thousand miles of shoreline in Willow Key."

Wyatt was right. This was a problem. We had no "com" and the GPS device was back in Jolene's Scorpion.

"She'll look for us or call for help on her radio," I said.

"Jolene, our *hero*," Shelby said.

"What's that supposed to mean?"

"What's the matter? You like her or something?" Shelby said.

"She's like *sixteen*." I said.

"Oh, whatever." Shelby turned away from me.

"But what if Jolene doesn't find us?" Bettina said.

"Someone will," I said without much behind it.

"But what if no one does?" Bettina looked worried.

I should have mentioned that Wyatt had a knife strapped to his leg. The reason I never brought it up before is that the rest of us kind of thought Wyatt was overdoing it on the gear. In movies and TV shows, divers use knives to fight off giant sharks or to disentangle themselves from the net of a fishing trawler that is really a launching pad for enemy missiles. In reality there is not much use for a knife when you are diving. If a shark decides to attack, you will be the last person on earth to know about it, and there aren't that many trawler/missile launchers prowling around. But Wyatt always strapped on a navy survival knife when he was out in the ocean, and now, as he pulled it from his sheath, it was as if all of those years of reading catalogs, diving manuals, and United States Navy survival guides had led him to this very moment.

Wyatt unscrewed a metal cap on the bottom of the knife; a fishing line, hook, and package of waterproof matches dropped into his hand.

"We're going to catch fish, cook them, and eat them," Wyatt said. "Now let's go collect some firewood."

Ty nodded at Wyatt. "Is good."

Wyatt grinned broadly. Compliments did not flow from Ty that often.

"What's that sound?" Bettina stood and squinted toward the horizon.

Far off in the distance we could see a tiny speck. It was Jolene's Chris Craft.

Wyatt leaped to his feet and began angling the shiny survival knife into the sun. Amazingly the knife reflected the sunlight, creating kind of a signal beacon. The engine noise grew louder as we all started jumping up and down on the beach hoping to catch Jolene's attention.

One or all of our techniques must have worked, because we watched the boat turn in our direction and pick up speed. The engine growled deeply as the boat neared shore. We were all overjoyed that we were going to be rescued. That is, until Jolene's boat, zigzagged wildly and FLIPPED OVER.

Shelby and I were first into the water. I promise I'm not bragging, but I'm the strongest swimmer of the Outriders. I reached the overturned boat first, just as Jolene popped her head above the surface. "You okay?" I yelled to her just as Shelby swam up alongside me.

"Manatee. I was going too fast, tried to swerve at the last second. Didn't hit him though." Jolene was treading water and a little out of breath as she spoke.

"Can we help you turn over the boat?" Shelby asked.

"You got a winch or a crane?"

"Maybe we can get the radio out of it," I said.

"Betcha it's kind of wet at the moment," Shelby said.

We then heard a gurgling sound. I looked over to see the Chris Craft Scorpion nose down and sink into Spider Bay.

"My mama's gonna kill me," Jolene said.

BEACHED

"You have any idea where we are?" Wyatt asked Jolene once she was safely on shore.

"Kinda. Put it this way: It would be a lot better if we were anywhere else."

"How come?" Shelby asked.

"There's nothin' here. The nearest road is a far ways from here and it's sorta *that way*." Jolene pointed into the dense mangrove forest.

Wyatt said, "You didn't happen to radio for help before the boat . . . ?"

"Nope."

There was a moment where everyone was thinking about our current problem. Pretty soon all eyes were on me.

I turned to Jolene and said, "Wyatt's got some fishing line and some matches. We could camp out here awhile."

"Even if y'all had rods, reels, and a bucket of night crawlers, that's a lousy idea."

"Why's that?" Wyatt almost looked insulted.

"The fish on this side of the Willow are fulla mercury. Y'all can catch as many as you want. Can't eat 'em, though."

"Your mom's fish camp is full of fisherman," Bettina said.

"They only fish on the east part of the Willow.

We're here smack dab on the west side—the poisonous side."

"Won't your mom get worried if you don't call in?" Shelby said.

"Yep. She'll worry. Problem is there's not much she can do about it. Even if she got all them fishermen out lookin' for us, it might take 'em a couple of weeks to look way over here."

Again, everyone turned to look at me.

"What choice do we have? We go *that way*," I said, pointing toward the mangrove forest.

"Problem," Wyatt said.

The day was getting hot and I was getting irritated. "What problem *now*, Wyatt?"

"We're going to have to abandon the gear." Wyatt was surveying the compressed air tanks, buoyancy compensator vests, scuba fins, and masks.

"And none of us except Jolene is wearing shoes," Bettina said.

She was right. We were all wearing scuba booties, which were like charcoal-gray neoprene socks. Jolene had a pair of soaking wet sneakers.

"It is what it is," I said, just to say something. I started pulling all the scuba gear toward the mangroves in order to hide it. "We'll stash this stuff here and try to come back for it later."

"Doesn't matter if you hide it or not. Nobody's gonna come by here one way or the other. We're sort of in the armpit of the Willow," Jolene said as she picked up El Trueno's sword and examined it. "This is way cool. Wanna tell me what happened to y'all down there?"

"Some wicked current dragged us toward this kind of narrow cave in the rocks," I said.

"The aquifer."

"What?"

"My mama warns me about it all the time. There's like rivers and lakes of water *underneath* the Willow."

"Water *under* the water?" Bettina said.

"Yeah, in like, deep caverns and stuff. It gets sucked in and out of all these holes. Y'all are lucky you're up here and not way, way down there."

All of us looked out at Spider Bay. I guessed that we were all imagining ourselves sucked into a deep underwater cavern.

"So, why are we standing around in the armpit of the Willow?" Shelby said.

I took a deep breath, took El Trueno's sword back

from Jolene, and headed toward the mangroves. I stopped to clip two of the plastic sample bottles to my swim trunks. I hadn't forgotten about that strange cement pipe we saw on the dive. Shelby, Bettina, Wyatt, Ty, and Jolene followed behind. We must have looked like a strange pirate crew—five middle schoolers wearing neon-colored rash guard shirts, bathing suits, and scuba booties with one sixteen-year-old country-and-western-singing river guide and her wet sneakers, hacking their way through the mangroves into the unknown.

CHAPTER EIGHT: BUSHWACKING

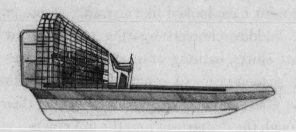

Remember how hot it was during the Mega-Wash? That day seemed like a cool spring rain compared to the temperature of Willow Key. Mangroves and saw-grass are both kind of short and stubby so they don't provide any shade, but they are just tall enough so that no breeze can penetrate.

ONE IMPORTANT MANGROVE FACT:

Mangroves have bumpy, knobby roots. These roots can extend four to five feet beyond the tree. They make walking really difficult, even if you have hiking boots, which none of us did.

ONE IMPORTANT SAW GRASS FACT:

Saw grass is a *sedge*, which means that the tall spiky plant has sharp edges that cut like razor blades if you brush against them.

ONE IMPORTANT WILDERNESS TIP:

If you find yourself walking in a mangrove/saw grass forest, try not to let the knobby-bumpy mangrove roots cause you to fall into the razor-sharp saw grass. It hurts; ask any of the six of us.

THE LONG MARCH

As morning turned into midafternoon, we began to find narrow trails cutting through the underbrush. These made walking much easier. The paths were just wide enough for us to march single file.

"Think someone lives around here?" I asked Jolene.

"Nope."

"Then these are deer paths?"

"Nope."

"What made them?"

"Wild boar."

Bettina's started swiveling her head around, alert for any movement. "Wild boars don't attack people, right?"

"Not as long as you obey one teeny rule," Jolene said.

"What rule is that?"

"Stay off their paths."

From that moment on, we became ultra-attuned to all the sounds of the Willow. Several times I thought I heard the distant squeal of a wild boar, but since I had no idea what a wild boar sounded like, it could have been the heat or my imagination.

A LIST OF ESSENTIALS FOR LONG HIKES:
1. Water
2. Food
3. Sun protection
4. Hiking shoes
5. Map/GPS device

LIST OF WHAT WE HAD:
1. Wyatt's navy survival knife
2. One fish hook
3. One strand nylon fishing line
4. Matches
5. A three-hundred-year-old Spanish sword with three diamond-shaped holes.

You would think that hiking eight hours through dense mangrove/saw grass forest without any water, food, or real shoes would have put *all* of us in a foul mood. But for some reason it only put *some* of us in a foul mood—the guys. Somehow Ty, Wyatt, and I ended up in front of the group and Shelby, Bettina, and Jolene were bringing up the rear.

Since the morning, Ty had been as silent as a stone. No, that's not 100 percent true. He did say, "I must to find wallet."

"Ty, your wallet is the least of our problems."

"Is important."

I was too sweaty and irritated to even respond. I just nodded. I looked over at Wyatt. He too was perspiring; actually the sweat was exploding from his forehead. In order to see, Wyatt kept wiping his eyes with the back of his hand. He had been doing this for so many hours that there was a stripe of red, irritated skin around his eyes and across the top of his nose. It gave Wyatt kind of a crazed-raccoon look. He caught me looking at him.

"What?"

"Nothing."

"Why are you staring?"

"I'm not."

"You are. Quit it."

Like I said, all the guys were ultra-grumpy.

But not the girls. Up until this morning, Shelby and Bettina did not seem to like Jolene at all. But ever since Jolene's boat sank into Spider Bay, the three of them seemed like best friends. My theory is that Jolene sort of *proved herself* when she came looking for us even though she didn't have to. From the moment Jolene emerged from the mucky water, Shelby and Bettina treated her as *one of us*. So for the past eight hours Shelby, Bettina, and Jolene had been *chatting*.

I was too busy trying to *survive* to overhear much of what the girls said, but I did catch some snippets. Jolene's father had remarried a woman who was a cat groomer. Jolene loved singing, but didn't think she "had whatchya need" to be a country-and-western star. Jolene thought guys who cut off the sleeves of their shirts to show off their muscles had "fish brains."

At one point I heard the three girls whispering. When they caught me looking back at them, Shelby, Bettina, and Jolene started *giggling*. There was a real chance that we were never going to make it out of Willow Key alive, but for some reason the three

156

girls were laughing, and apparently the laughter had something to do with *me*.

I will be the first to admit, many things about girls confuse me. When you surf, you learn really quickly that the ocean is unpredictable. You can sit on your board for two hours and not catch a single wave, and then all of a sudden, without any warning, a huge set of five footers comes out of nowhere. But the randomness of the sea is nothing compared to trying to decipher why three girls plodding along a wild boar trail in a mangrove forest are giggling at you.

I didn't have enough energy to spend time thinking about it. The sun had started to go down and I hadn't eaten since early that morning. I had been ravenously hungry for the entire day, but now the hunger was taking on a new dimension. I could put up with the strange behavior of my friends, I could deal with the dozens of cuts all over my arms and legs from the saw grass blades, I could even cope with the Jurassic Park–like heat, but my need to eat was driving me *insane*. All I could think about was pizza. I tried to push all pizza thoughts from my head, but my brain wouldn't let me. I found myself imagining all my favorite toppings: pepperoni, sausage, extra cheese, garlic, onions, olives, and hot peppers. I even thought about the time Shelby ordered a ham-and-pineapple pizza from Starlight Pizzeria. We had given her a hard time about it until we all took a slice and found out it tasted really, really good. Pineapple, ham, and pizza shouldn't work together, but they do. The sweet of the pineapple and the saltiness of the ham tasted really delicious together. I vowed that if I made it out of Willow Key alive, I would order another one of those pizzas. They called it a Luau Special. The word *luau* is weird, when you think about it. Are there any other words with "uau" all together like that? I must have been starting to hallucinate, because I actually *smelled* ham cooking. I had clearly lost my mind, because I definitely smelled delicious ham. Ham is kind of a funny word too. I was even hearing things; I heard *engines*—big engines. Almost like the propellers on Mr. Thorpe's seaplane. *Seaplane* is a funny word.

Shelby said, "What's that noise?"

I guess I wasn't imagining things; there was real engine noise! And I'm pretty sure there was a real ham smell as well!

Wyatt pumped his fist in the air. "We made it!" He started to run in the direction of the sounds. That's when Jolene stuck out her foot and tripped him.

"HEY!" Wyatt said.

Jolene put a finger up to her lips as if to say, *Be quiet.* Then she helped Wyatt to his feet and motioned for us to follow behind her. She moved cautiously in the direction of the engine noise, making sure to crouch below the tops of the mangroves so as not to be seen. As we all moved forward, the mechanical roar got louder and louder. All of a sudden Jolene stopped and crouched down behind a thicket of mangroves. We all knelt down behind her.

The sun had almost disappeared. The shadows were deepening behind the mangroves. In the gray half-light it was hard to make out the faces of my friends—that is, until a BRIGHT WHITE SHAFT OF LIGHT pierced through the leaves of the mangroves.

Jolene pushed us all down to the ground. We hid ourselves below the thick tangle of mangrove roots as the white light moved in an arc away from us. It reminded me of one of those prison movies where the guard tower searchlights scan the perimeter fence looking for escapees.

Shelby whispered to Jolene, "What is that?"

"Look," Jolene whispered back.

Jolene pushed aside a thick mangrove branch and

we all peered through the opening. The first things I noticed were the airboats. There were three of them in the water, each with an enormous search-light mounted on the bow of the boat. I don't know if you have ever seen an airboat, but try to picture a huge airplane propeller that is surrounded by a protective cage and is mounted on the back of a flat-bottomed boat. Then picture the propeller pushing the boat across the shallow water at around thirty-five miles an hour. Also try to imagine how LOUD an airplane propeller would sound if you were kneeling really close to it. The engines of the three boats were ROARING as they started to pull away from shore.

Next I noticed the men on the boats. I don't know why I knew they were dangerous (maybe the machetes they all carried), but instinctively I was certain these weren't men that would be interested in rescuing a bunch of middle schoolers and their sixteen-year-old guide.

"Who are *they*?" I whispered to Jolene.

"The last people you ever want to run into," Jolene said.

Her face was motionless, her eyes narrowed. I didn't know her well enough to guess what she was feeling, but I knew it didn't include "happy."

I looked at the lead boat. The guy piloting it was tall and heavy, like a jock who used to play football in high school but then just sat in front of the TV eating potato chips for twenty years. Instead of a baseball cap he wore a red, white, and blue bandana. I was about thirty feet away from him, but even from that distance I could see that he was missing a couple of teeth on one side of his mouth. This gave him a kind of a freaky lopsided smile.

Jolene tapped me on the forearm and whispered, "That there is Gorman Turley."

"Who's he?"

Before Jolene could answer the three airboats turned away from our position and a massive *backwash* of air tornadoed right at us. We were all hit with a spray of water and dirt, forcing us to close our eyes until the boats pushed off down the inland waterway.

"You wanna know who Gorman Turley is? Take a look-see."

I opened my eyes. Now that the airboats and their huge lights were gone, I got my first good look at Gorman Turley's camp. What I saw was the most horrible thing I've ever seen in my whole life. It made me sick to my stomach. I heard Shelby and Bettina gasp.

Across the waterway in front of us were the drying skins of dozens of dead alligators. The "ham" smell was actually the smoldering embers of a charcoal fire, which I guess was used to speed up the "drying" of the gator skins. What used to be alligators were hanging by their tails, suspended from a wooden frame. The skins twisted on nylon ropes, pushed by a slight breeze. There were flies buzzing around the dead reptiles, and now that the airboats had departed, we could hear their steady buzz of sadness.

"My mama's been after that poacher for *years*. Never once caught him in the act," Jolene said.

"But now we can bring your mom back here and show her Gorman Turley's camp," Bettina said.

"Problem," Wyatt said.

Everyone turned to look at Wyatt. We all understood we had to somehow make it back to civilization before we could tell Rita Mae about the poachers.

"Sorry," Wyatt said.

In biology class, Mr. Mora was always talking about how all life on earth is connected by a "fragile chain." Mr. Mora says that we as human beings are supposed to be responsible for protecting each individual "living link." I had only seen Gorman Turley for about a minute, but I knew for a fact that he had taken his machete and hacked right through the "fragile chain." I found myself clenching my fists. My face felt tight, my breathing shallow. I now understood what Jolene had been feeling. It was hatred.

ONE IMPORTANT THING ABOUT ME

I'm one of those people who doesn't throw the word *hate* around. It is an ultra-harsh word. My mom picked up and left the family when I was a little boy. My father and brother won't even answer my questions about her. When I think about her, I get sad or disappointed, sometimes even angry. But, wherever she is, I don't *hate* my mother. So hating someone doesn't come naturally to me. But when I looked across the now inky black water at all those poor alligators, I knew for certain I hated Gorman Turley. And that's why it didn't bother me at all that I was going to steal his airboat.

NOT SCAVENGING

"Where are you going?" Wyatt shrieked as he saw me wading across the small stretch of water toward Gorman's camp.

I didn't bother to reply. I had my mission and I wasn't going to be deterred.

The water was really shallow, so it was easy to make it across. For some reason I wasn't worried about encountering any alligators in the water. Maybe I should have been freaked out, but I was counting on the fact that most alligators would be smart enough to avoid sloshing around a poacher's camp.

I also should have been worried that some of Gorman's men would still be in the camp. But I saw absolutely no signs of anyone being around.

Sometimes I surf during a big winter swell. The waves get really steep and insanely dangerous. The most important thing to be when you are surfing the big waves is *decisive*. You can't start paddling to catch a ride on a ten-foot wave and say to yourself, "Should I drop in now or maybe two seconds from now?" You just have to *go*. I think Shelby, Bettina, Wyatt, Ty, and Jolene sensed I had decided to "drop into" something, and they followed me across the waterway even though they had no idea what I was planning.

A few seconds later I reached the airboat. The poachers had taken three boats but left one beached at the camp. A bunch of dried-out alligator skins were stretched across one of the metal bench seats at the front of the airboat. They were held in place by bungee cords. The eyes of the lifeless reptiles seemed to be staring up at me.

I checked the boat for a radio. There was none. I refused to even consider the possibility that this airboat was broken or couldn't be started. I turned to face Jolene.

"Can you drive this thing?"

"Yep. But this boat might be broke."

Suddenly the airboat engine ROARED to life. Wyatt, who had already climbed on board, looked over at us with a huge smile ripping across his face. "They left the key in it!"

I looked at Jolene. "I guess they don't put antitheft devices on airboats."

Jolene shook her head. "That's 'cause nobody'd be a big enough fool to steal Gorman Turley's boat!"

Ty began helping Shelby and Bettina onto one of the bench seats behind the alligator skins. "Must not to stay here," was all he said.

I told you that when Ty speaks, everyone tends to listen.

Jolene traded places with Wyatt. She took the lone "captain's chair" at the rear of the boat just in front of the huge propeller. I took the position at the very front of the boat so I could operate the searchlight. I needed both hands free, and I realized I was still carrying El Trueno's sword. I pulled the back of my rashguard shirt collar away from my neck and slipped the sword down the length of my back. Luckily the years underwater had dulled the edges, otherwise I would have sliced myself to pieces. The hilt of the sword rested snugly against my shoulder. It occurred to me that I was carrying a pirate sword while I was stealing Gorman Turley's boat. I pushed that thought away as I clicked on the massive searchlight. It lit up Gorman Turley's camp like the sun.

"They use those lights to attract the alligators," Wyatt said to me as he sat down. "Then they toss this stuff in the water."

I looked into a white plastic bucket to my right. It was filled with raw chicken parts and gooey red stuff that I guessed was chicken blood.

"The only thing we're using this light for is to find a way out of here," I said.

Shelby started to unhook the bungee cords from the gator skins.

"Don't y'all do that! We need them skins!" Jolene shouted from the captain's chair. "If I get those to my mama, Gorman Turley goes to jail!"

Bettina helped Shelby reattach the bungee cords as Jolene navigated the airboat into the waterway.

I thought about Din, Nar, and Mr. Mora back at base camp. By this time they must have been really worried about us. I was the one who'd insisted that we stay down in Willow Key. It was because I wanted to dive the wreck of *L'Esperanza*. If I had enough time to think about it, I would feel really awful, but I was focused on helping us get out of the armpit of the Willow.

It was fully dark by this time, but the powerful searchlight lit the way. Jolene was fairly expert at handling the airboat. I watched her blond hair fluttering in the breeze. I must have been ultra-thirsty because I had some trouble swallowing.

"You know the way back to Hammock Landing?" Wyatt yelled to Jolene.

"Maybe," was all she said.

"She'll figure it out," Shelby said to Wyatt.

"Absolutely," Bettina said; then she added, "Jolene rocks."

Wyatt, Ty, and I glanced at each other. I could tell that they realized even here, in the remote backwater of Willow Key, we three guys were playing catch-up with a group of very fast-moving girls. We didn't necessarily understand what was going on, but it wasn't a new sensation for us.

With no warning, Ty leaped over the benches in front of him, pushed me aside, and clicked off the searchlight.

"Hey, sad boy! I can't see!" Jolene yelled from the stern.

"Is not good," Ty whispered to me, and pointed ahead.

That's when I saw three powerful searchlights arcing across the water in front of us. Then Gorman Turley's boat rounded the bend of the waterway. The other two boats followed closely behind. Within an instant their searchlights found our boat. We were lit up in a blaze of white-hot light! All of us squinted and held hands up in front of our eyes.

"Must to run!" Ty yelled to Jolene.

"DUH!" Was the only word Jolene said as she gunned the throttle and turned the boat in the opposite direction.

I immediately clicked back on our searchlight to light the way. I looked back. We still had several hundred yards on Turley and his men, but they were closing fast. They had every advantage. Each of their three boats contained only two men, ours had six (even if most of us were much smaller). Also, they knew these waters. Jolene was just improvising. Most importantly, we were going to have to get very, very lucky to escape, and they needed little or no luck to ram our airboat and send us all into the inky blackness of Spider Bay.

Jolene did rock. She was pushing the airboat full bore on one of the channels that snaked around fields of saw grass. Turley and his men actually lost ground for a few moments.

Jolene made a hairpin turn around a bend in the channel, and for a few brief moments we couldn't see Turley's searchlights behind us.

"You know where this channel leads?" I heard Wyatt scream to Jolene above the roar of the propeller.

"No clue!" She yelled back.

Since I was manning the searchlight, I was the first to notice that the channel was getting narrower. Also I noticed that the mangrove trees and saw grass were starting to disappear. Large, twisted cypress trees dripping with garlands of light green moss were now lining the channel. Jolene was forced to zigzag through the boughs of the trees. Huge protruding cypress "knees" jutted into the water, further slowing our progress.

We now heard Turley and his men gaining on us. Their searchlights cast eerie shadows through the gnarled limbs of the cypress trees.

BWAM! The metal hull of the airboat slammed against a partially submerged cypress knee. The hidden stump acted like a ramp and the six of us were almost tossed from the boat as it went airborne. Miraculously Jolene managed to straighten our vessel and continue darting through the trees.

The water beneath us was thick with vegetation. In the beam of the searchlight I could see the yellow eyes of alligators peering just over the surface of the water. I am not Mr. Biology, but it was clear we were moving deeper and deeper into the belly of a DENSE SWAMP.

"What is this place?" Bettina yelled to Jolene.

"La Muerta Verde."

Everyone looked to Shelby for the translation.

"'The Green Death.'"

That horrifying thought hung in the air for a moment until Gorman Turley's searchlights had targeted us again. We discovered that Turley and his men were now only about sixty yards behind us!

"They must have flipped off their lights!" I yelled.

One of Turley's boats zoomed forward. It sliced through the cypress trees like an Olympic skier going through the slalom gates. Jolene sensed the approach of the boat and tried to make tighter turns around the trees, but since she wasn't familiar with this part of the Willow, she was only guessing about where to make her turns. Each time our flat-bottomed boat was banged against a submerged cypress knee, there was an explosive metallic BANG that echoed throughout the swamp.

Our nearest pursuer was now almost nose to tail with our airboat. Their plan was clear. They intended to bump us into one of the cypress trees. I could clearly see the poacher at the prow of the air-boat in the reflected glow of the searchlight. He was laughing at us.

I noticed Ty picking up the white plastic bucket of chicken parts. It was a ten-gallon bucket, but Ty lifted it as if it were a Styrofoam cup. From his position in the middle of the boat, Ty HEAVED the bucket toward the airboat chasing us. Ty made sure to launch it high enough to clear Jolene's head.

Still, Jolene had to duck in her captain's chair as the ten-gallon bucket flew over her and scored a direct hit on Turley's man at the prow of the boat.

Five things happened in rapid succession. Turley's man was knocked backward into the metal bench behind him. The searchlight he was holding swiveled 180 degrees and ended up pointing DIRECTLY AT THE PILOT. Blinded by the powerful light, the airboat pilot yanked his control stick violently, and the airboat rammed against a cypress tree. The nose of the boat actually climbed up the tree, so for a moment the boat became vertical. Then the enormous propeller at the rear became submerged and chopped at the water like some type of titan-size blender. I saw both men jump into the water. I wondered if any of the yellow-eyed alligators were around to witness it.

One of Turley's boats slowed to pick up their friends while Turley himself closed in on us. In the glow of his searchlight I could see his freakish grin. That was frightening enough, but not as frightening as Turley's abrupt change of plan. He slowed his boat to a crawl. Jolene rocketed ours seventy yards into the lead. Was Turley giving up? It didn't seem likely. I looked forward. The searchlight illuminated my answer. We were running out of swamp.

About a hundred yards in the distance I saw a cultivated field of some kind.

I yelled to Jolene, "Is that a cornfield?

She yelled back, "Sugarcane."

Just like when I was surfing the big swell, my mind was amazingly clear. "GUN IT!"

"ARE YOU CRAZY?"

"GUN IT!"

For some crazy reason, Jolene did as I said and pushed the throttle to the limit. We were heading on a collision course for the sugarcane field.

I reached down and grabbed the navy survival knife from the scabbard on Wyatt's leg. I unscrewed the bottom of the knife and grabbed the waterproof matches.

"TAKE THE LIGHT!" I yelled to Wyatt. Wyatt grabbed the searchlight handle and kept it focused on the sugarcane field.

I started hurdling over the metal bench seats back toward Jolene. We were only seconds from leaving the water and launching ourselves into the field. I took the razor-sharp knife and plunged it into the gas tank of the airboat. A jet stream of gasoline began whipping out of the tank.

Jolene's eyes went wide. She must have thought I had gone psycho or something.

"HOLD ON!" Jolene shouted as the boat ramped up the small bank next to the cane field. We left the water and began hurtling into the air. We launched about twenty yards into the sugarcane field when the flat-bottomed boat came to earth with an ear-splitting THUD and crashed through the stalks of sugarcane, the massive propeller pushing us deeper into the leafy green stalks. Somehow, maybe because we had all death-gripped ourselves to the boat, we managed to stay aboard.

"RUN!" I yelled.

Everyone leaped off the airboat and ran into the sugarcane. I stayed for only a few seconds to strike a match and light the gasoline pouring out of the airboat tank. I heard a small *whoosh* but didn't see any flame. I remembered when Wyatt's hair had caught fire. There was no visible flame. I didn't wait around; I dove into the sugarcane and ran as fast as I could, trampling the stalks in front of me. The massive explosion sent me sprawling into Bettina and Shelby. We all crashed down in a pile. I looked around and saw Jolene, Ty, and Wyatt crouched in the cane beside us. There was now a huge fire raging on what used to be the airboat. Some of the stalks of sugarcane were also on fire and the air was thick with black choking smoke, the smell of gasoline, and just a hint of something sweet, like caramel. The flames of the fireball reached fifty feet into the sky.

Shelby looked at me. "El Trueno! You brought the thunder!"

"KEEP RUNNING!" I shouted as we all got to our feet and pushed farther into the cane field.

I turned to Jolene. "What was the name of that forest ranger in the tower?"

"Varsha Patel."

"Let's hope she's on duty," I said as we ran from the flames.

CHAPTER NINE: CAPTURING

It didn't take long for Gorman Turley's two remaining airboats to arrive. After their engines turned off, we heard Turley shouting to his men.

Here's the thing about running through a cane field: You would think it would be easy to hide in all the tall sugarcane, but the flattened stalks that you've pushed through are like easy-to-follow footprints. Shelby, Bettina, Wyatt, Ty, Jolene, and I were like a herd of crazed yaks knocking down everything in our path. We realized very quickly we needed a new plan if we were going to escape.

The cane field seemed endless. As we were running, I noticed that every fifty yards or so there were metal plates, like square manhole covers set into the ground. As we reached the next one of these, I held up my hand as if to say *Stop*.

Ty reached down and lifted the heavy metal plate. Below us we saw what looked like a round cement well. The well wasn't very deep, and it only had about three or four inches of yellow-brown water at the bottom. The well was like the hub of a wheel and four cement pipes radiated out from the center like spokes. Each pipe was about three feet in diameter. I assumed that this well-and-pipe junction must have been part of the irrigation system of the cane field.

We heard voices very close behind us. We didn't hesitate; all six of us jumped into the cement well. Once inside, Ty lifted the heavy metal plate and slid it back over the opening, careful to not make any noise. A light clicked on. Wyatt, the king of gear, was holding his underwater flashlight. We all heard footsteps pounding near the metal plate. I pointed to one of the pipes and Wyatt crawled inside. Wyatt's small size made him an ideal tunnel leader and we all shimmied in behind him. Ty was the largest, so he brought up the rear.

We heard the metal plate being lifted off the well.

A shaft of moonlight appeared at the end of the tunnel. Without pausing, we kept crawling on our hands and knees farther into the darkness. We heard Turley yelling into the well.

"Y'all can't stay down there forever, boys and girls!"

Then the metal plate clanged down in place and the moonlight disappeared. Now our only point of reference was the beam of Wyatt's underwater flashlight as he pushed into the dark abyss of the tunnel.

Here's the thing about crawling on your hands and knees in a tunnel: It hurts. All of us had already been sliced up by the saw grass, our feet were killing us from the eight-hour hike in the scuba booties, we were thirsty, hungry, and exhausted, and now our palms and knees were being sanded down to the bone by the cement pipe. Also the yellow-brown liquid that trickled below us smelled rancid.

I noticed that Wyatt had stopped crawling. We all bunched up behind him. He had reached another one of the round well structures. Above us was another metal plate. We didn't hear anything above us, but I couldn't take any chances.

I whispered, "We can't make it this easy on them." I pointed to the pipe that angled off at ninety degrees to the one that we were in. "We have to zigzag so they don't know where we are coming out."

Bettina looked as if she'd given up hope. "How long are we going to be crawling around down here?"

"For as long as it takes," I said.

Wyatt led the way into the second tunnel. I may have been imagining things, but it seemed as if his flashlight batteries had weakened; the beam of light seemed dimmer.

I'm not bragging, but I have a really good sense of direction. When I go to a new place—like a hike I've never taken before—a kind of map grid pops into my brain, and I find it easy to make the hike and get back to where I started with very little problem. Even here in the dark cement tunnels, I was envisioning a map grid. I was keeping mental track of the ninety-degree turns we were taking so that we wouldn't double back on ourselves. Our crawling went on for what seemed like an eternity. Finally we got to our ninth or tenth well structure and we noticed shafts of dim light peeking through the edges of the metal plate.

"Getting near morning." Wyatt stated the obvious again.

I could feel the blade of El Trueno's sword pressing against my back. It felt like there was going to be a permanent ridge running down my shoulder blade that would mark me forever.

"Is this the same stuff that was coming out of the pipe near the wreck?" Bettina was looking down at the yellow-brown trickle of water running through the cement pipe.

"It seems like it's the same color," I said.

"My daddy used to work in a cane field. Never saw no pipe system like this," Jolene said.

"This stuff smells." Wyatt and the obvious, yet again.

"Fertilizer," Jolene said.

Ty started to stand. He was just about to slide the metal plate off of the well structure.

"Wait," I said.

"You think they're still looking for us?" Shelby peered up at the metal plate separating us from the sunlight.

Jolene answered before I could. "Count on it."

Shelby thought for a moment. "This is a farm, right? It has to be near a road."

"That's the first place Turley and his guys will look for us," I said.

"We can't stay down here forever!" Shelby was frustrated like the rest of us.

And she was right. We couldn't stay down in the pipes forever. Our only hope was that our zig-zagging had put us in a spot far from Turley and his men so we could make a run for it. What direction we would run, or where we would run to, was something we'd just have to figure out at the moment.

I nodded at Ty. Ty carefully lifted the metal plate and gently slid it to the side. Pale morning light flooded into the well. Slowly Ty raised his head into the fresh air and came face-to-face with a blood-hound.

"Good girl, Jezebel," Gorman Turley said. "Now y'all climb out of there. Ain't no place for little children."

Jezebel, the bloodhound, wasn't growling or snarling. In fact she was wagging her tail. But she was the only friendly face in the vicinity. When I looked up from the well, Gorman and his five men were glaring down at us. One of the men, the one who was manning the searchlight when Ty threw the bucket of chicken, was completely drenched in red chicken blood.

"Is bad," Ty mumbled as we all climbed out of the well.

"Gorman Turley, my mama's gonna put you in

jail!" That was the first thing Jolene said when she climbed out of the hole.

"Lookee here, ain't that Rita Mae Thibodaux's little girl?" one of Gorman's men said.

"I asked your mama to go out with me in high school," Gorman said to Jolene. "She turned me down flat."

"My mama's no fool."

"But her little girly sure is." Gorman parted his lips to reveal his eerie smile.

The six of us were standing at the edge of the cement well. We had somehow crawled through enough tunnels that we were out of the cane field and standing in a clearing bordered by more cypress trees. Turley and his five men were in a circle around us. If we all scattered, possibly one or two of us could make it back into the cane field, but where would we run to? In the distance I could see a small shack that might have been a farmhouse.

"I radioed her, Gorman. She's coming for us," Jolene said.

"That's a nice bluff, but they ain't made a radio yet that would reach your mama all the way over there in Hammock Landing. You're on the far side of the moon now, girly."

I looked toward the small shack and started waving as if saying hello to an old friend. Turley and his men glanced away briefly, then looked back at me.

"You sick in the head, boy?" Turley said to me.

"I saw the cane farmer over there. Thought I'd wave hello."

Turley and his men started laughing.

"I'm sure the farm owner will be calling the police when he sees all of you on his land."

"Sonny boy, you're talkin' to the owner of this property. This here's Turley land, and y'all are trespassin'."

"Oh," was all I could manage as a reply.

It was a pitiful bluff on my part. But it was the only plan I had. I felt my friends looking in my direction, hoping I would come up with something. But I didn't see any way out. I felt empty, like all the air had left my body. I had planned the Mega-Wash; I had insisted we stay in Willow Key after Mr. Mora broke his ankle; I had decided to push into the mangrove forest; and, because of me, my friends and I were surrounded by the most dangerous-looking bunch of machete-carrying poachers the world has ever seen. I looked around at the scared faces of my friends and realized I was responsible for all that had happened.

"A lot of people are looking for us," I said with absolutely nothing behind it.

"But they won't find you," Gorman Turley said. "Gators don't leave no crumbs."

All my muscles tightened. I felt the cold steel of El Trueno's sword pressing against my back. It was as if the ancient pirate was sending me some type of signal.

In one swift motion I reached up above my shoulder, grabbed the hilt of El Trueno's sword, and pulled it from beneath my neon black and yellow rash-guard shirt. I brandished the sword menacingly and advanced toward Turley. I was determined that I would use the ancient pirate's weapon to bring down this modern-day poacher. I took a mighty swing with the sword. In a flash, Gorman Turley whipped off his red, white, and blue bandana and snagged the end of the sword in the fabric. He then shoved hard on the blade, knocking me backward. In the blink of an eye he had the sword pointed right at my chest.

I felt my heart pounding. It was pounding so hard that I even *heard* it. Thump, thump, thump. It must have been loud enough for Shelby to hear, because she cocked her head in a funny way. But that didn't make sense. How could she hear my pounding heart? Then I realized Shelby was looking toward the sky. Turley and his men glanced over their shoulders. The thumping noise got louder and LOUDER as an enormous orange United States Coast Guard Jayhawk helicopter landed in the clearing.

Before Turley and his men could run, ten United States Coast Guardsmen sprang out of the copter. I saw Petty Officer First Class Kevin Doherty and his huge shoulders step off the helicopter followed by Rita Mae, Mr. Mora (on crutches), Din, Nar, and finally 243-pound Howie.

At that moment, Gorman Turley and his men made two decisions that they would regret for a long, long time:

1. Turley's man, the one who was covered in chicken blood (I found out his name was Enos), made the mistake of grabbing Bettina as if trying to take a hostage. One millisecond later, Enos was TACKLED by a flying Timor Dymincyzk. Ty didn't play on the football team; he was operating on pure protective

instinct. Enos did not know what hit him. He still had the wind knocked out of him when the Coast Guardsmen handcuffed him.

2. Gorman Turley, still holding El Trueno's sword, decided to RUN, but that *wasn't* his big mistake. As fate would have it, Nar Bonglukiet was standing between Turley and the protection of the cane field. As Turley ran past Nar, he shoved him out of the way, knocking Nar over. *That* was the mistake that would haunt Turley's dreams.

You can stick your hand in Howie's food bowl while he's eating; he doesn't care. A little kid can yank on Howie's tail; it doesn't bother him. But if you are foolish enough to harm one of the Bonglukiet twins, you are going to have to deal with Howie.

Turley was fast. He managed to sprint through all of the Coast Guardsmen and made it to the sugarcane field. He disappeared into the bright green stalks. He might have been able to escape had he not knocked over Howie's master.

Howie took only two massive strides to reach full speed. From that point on he became a 243-pound tan-colored locomotive with teeth. None of us saw what happened next; we only *heard* it. Howie disappeared into the sugarcane field at the exact same spot that Turley had entered it. We watched as the tips of the cane disappeared, trampled by the angry mastiff. Then we heard a high-pitched human scream. Then SILENCE.

All of the outriders, Petty Officer Doherty, Rita Mae, and two Coast Guard officers ran into the cane field, following the flattened stalks of sugar cane. About sixty yards into the field we found Gorman Turley flat on his stomach with a 243-pound dog sitting on his back. Howie was holding El Trueno's pirate sword in his mouth, as if he had found a new and interesting toy to play with. Gorman was in obvious pain, but he wasn't making a sound. He had no intention of angering the mastiff. He looked almost grateful when Kevin Doherty handcuffed him and Nar told Howie to "*maa*" (which means "come" in Thai).

By this time Rita Mae had pulled Jolene into a big hug.

"How'd you find us, Mama?"

"You were missin'. Varsha Patel spotted a fire. We figured two and two added up to you six, so here we are."

"I sunk our boat."

"We'll find it. Don't you never mind."

Din, Nar, and Howie walked over to Ty. Ty patted Howie's enormous head.

"Is hero, Howie," Ty said.

Nar broke out in a huge smile. If you compliment Howie, you are complimenting Nar. It's that simple.

Din reached into his pocket, pulled out a wallet, and showed it to Ty. "Nar and I found it."

Ty took the wallet, opened it, and checked something inside. I can't be sure, but it seemed like there were tears at the corners of his eyes. He reached down and lifted both Bonglukiet twins into the air.

"You heroes!"

Jolene turned to me and said, "That sad kid is strange."

I smiled. "Only I'm allowed to say that, but today you get a pass."

Mr. Mora had clomped through the cane field on his crutches and approached me. By this time, I was holding El Trueno's sword. Mr. Mora took it from me. He examined every inch of it.

"This is incredible."

"Shelby solved the mystery of El Trueno's sword."

Mr. Mora looked up at me. "We were worried. Really worried."

"So were we," I said.

"You'll have to tell me all about it on the plane ride home."

"What about your research?"

Mr. Mora laughed and put his hand on my shoulder. "Cam, it really doesn't seem that important anymore."

I held up the Nalgene plastic sample bottle that was clipped to my bathing suit. "But this might be."

CHAPTER TEN: ROUND-TRIPPING

Helicopters are wicked cool. If someone offers you a chance for a ride in a Coast Guard Jayhawk helicopter, don't walk, run. It is *that* impressive.

I sat next to Mr. Mora during takeoff. Out the window I could see the burned-up shell of the airboat we'd stolen from Gorman Turley. Then I got a look at La Muerta Verde from the air. I couldn't believe Jolene had actually navigated her way through that swamp—at night.

As we swung out past the Green Death, Jolene made sure to point out Gorman Turley's poacher camp to her mother. The Coast Guard navigator took down the coordinates in his onboard computer.

I was sitting on a jump seat between Mr. Mora and Petty Officer Doherty. I downloaded the entire expedition to both of them. I made sure to tell them about the dead reef, the strange cement pipe, the sucking vortex of the aquifer, and the yellow-brown stuff we saw at the sugarcane field.

Mr. Mora was interested in everything I had to say, but he looked really upset. I asked him why.

"I brought all of you down here. This has all been my fault."

"Mr. Mora, it's *my* fault."

"I'm the teacher."

"And you saved our lives."

"No, Cam, it was you who did that. You started that fire."

"That was just lucky."

Petty Officer First Class Kevin Doherty looked over at me. "You make your own luck, soldier."

For the first time in many, many hours I felt pretty good. Also Petty Officer Doherty had called me "soldier," which was cool.

Petty Officer Doherty put his hand on my shoulder. "You've got to do me one big favor."

"Anything, sir."

"Go home."

BACK IN THE HAMMOCK

By the time the Jayhawk helicopter landed back at Rita Mae's Fish Camp, all the other kids from our class had already returned from Osprey Grove campsite. All of our backpacks and gear (except for the scuba stuff we had abandoned) had been squared away and made ready for travel. Mr. Thorpe's PBY was waiting just offshore to take us home.

As soon as we disembarked from the Jayhawk, Mr. Mora rushed over to one of the cases that held his scientific equipment. He clicked open the latches and took out the mercury testing kit. He then dipped a pipette into the Nalgene sample bottle we had given him. He carefully went through the procedure with the chemicals and the nitrogen gas balloon.

And nothing happened. The clear balloon did not turn orange. There was no mercury in the sample.

By this time all of the Outriders had crowded around our biology teacher. We had believed that the mysterious yellow-brown fertilizer was the cause of all the mercury poisoning in Willow Key. I looked around at my friends. We all looked sad, like we had failed Mr. Mora in some way.

Then we heard humming. The humming was coming from Mr. Mora. He was busy taking some brown bottles of chemicals that we hadn't seen before out of his equipment case. He poured some clear liquids into a beaker. Soon Mr. Mora began softly singing. I recognized the song. It was the same one Jolene had sung when we arrived.

> Don't ever pick a fight with a grizzly bear.
> Don't you corner a badger, they don't fight fair.
> Don't grab a cougar's tail and give it a whirl.
> And don't you ever, ever lie to a country girl.

A bunch of us started laughing. The song sounded very ridiculous coming from Mr. Mora. Rita Mae and Jolene came over to see what all the commotion was about.

"He got himself some heatstroke?" Rita Mae said.

"Mr. Mora, what's going on?" Wyatt said.

Mr. Mora dropped a sample of the yellow-brown liquid into the beaker. It turned a deep red. He looked up for a moment, smiled at all of us and said, "Time for some more biology."

BIOLOGY 102

"No one was ever dumping any mercury!"

We all stood in a tight circle looking at Mr. Mora. Obviously he was hurtling along on a very exciting train of thought. None of us were on the same train, however.

"I kept looking for mercury, when there *was no mercury*!"

"But . . . the orange balloons? You said it meant there was mercury in Spider Bay, right?" I was deeply, deeply confused.

"But no one was dumping it! I don't know how I couldn't have seen it."

"Mr. Mora, how could there be mercury if no one is putting it there?" Shelby was as confused as I was and she had gotten straight As in biology (and every other subject).

"*Mercury* is everywhere. It occurs naturally. *Methyl mercury* is what you have to worry about. It's deadly."

"So someone is dumping *methyl* mercury?" Din asked.

"That's what I thought and that's why I couldn't ever figure it out!" Mr. Mora pointed to the red liquid in the beaker. "That sample you collected is raw, untreated *fertilizer*. And you know what happens when you dump fertilizer into the ecosystem without treating it first?"

"It turns into methyl mercury?" Nar said what we were all thinking.

"No, it doesn't. But it does cause a bloom of sulfate reducing bacteria. And sulfate reducing bacteria is what turns the good, naturally occurring mercury into methyl mercury!"

My brain was going into overload. "Hold on. You mean the sugarcane fertilizer from Gorman Turley's farm caused some bacteria to grow in the water, and that bacteria was the stuff that made the poisonous kind of mercury?"

"That's right! And the methyl mercury was getting sucked back into the aquifer. Turley was poisoning the groundwater as well as the bay. That's why there are no willows in Willow Key. The willows are supersensitive to mercury. You guys solved the mystery! We now know why Willow Key was dying."

Bettina said, "So Turley isn't just a *poacher*, he's a *polluter*?"

"Now he's neither. He's just a prisoner," Rita Mae said triumphantly.

Mr. Mora handed Rita Mae a card. "If you need me to testify, I'm available."

Rita Mae smiled as she looked at the card. "I might be calling on you, Mr. Peter Mora."

"Next time you see him it might be *Doctor* Peter Mora," I said.

I heard the engines of the PBY begin to roar. All of us picked up our backpacks.

Rita Mae and Jolene ferried the whole group of us out to the seaplane.

As I was getting off her boat, I said to Jolene, "Don't give up singing. You're awesome." I realized I sounded like one of those idiot TV friends who says the really supportive thing.

Jolene looked right into my eyes. "You crushin' on me, Cam Walker?"

I almost choked. "Uh . . . no, I . . . uh, meant that . . ."

Jolene started laughing. "I'm just bustin' chops, junior. Try to keep up or you'll get left behind."

Then Jolene tousled my hair and pushed me into the seaplane.

A few minutes later all the gear was stowed. I sat down. There was an open seat next to me. Bettina walked right past and moved closer to Ty.

"This seat taken?"

Ty smiled broadly. "Not taken," he said.

As Bettina sat down next to Ty, Shelby plopped down next to me.

I looked over toward Ty. He had pulled out his wallet and was showing Bettina a black-and-white photo preserved in a clear plastic flap.

I heard Bettina say, "Who's that?"

"Mother of me."

Bettina looked at the photo for a long moment. "She's beautiful."

"Only picture of her." Ty held the wallet as carefully as if it were a small injured bird.

"Where is your mom?"

Ty remained silent.

"Did she . . . ?"

Ty just nodded.

"I'm so sorry, Ty. Was she sick?"

Ty shook his head.

"What happened?"

"In my country. War."

Bettina didn't say anything. She just put her hand on top of Ty's. In that moment I thought she was the nicest person in the whole world.

Ty knew that the rest of us had overheard him. He hadn't said very many words, but he told us all something very important. It wasn't just Bettina that he would lay down his life for; it was all of us, the Outriders. The weirdness between all of us had bothered Ty more than anyone else, because Ty was afraid that it would break apart the group. He'd already had enough loss. He didn't want to deal with more. I'm not some deep psychological thinker or anything. But I knew I was right about Ty because I felt the exact same way. Maybe kids who are missing a parent need their friends more than other kids. I'm not sure. I know it is true for me.

Shelby pointed to something on my shirt. "What is this drool?"

I looked down. Shelby lifted her finger, and smacked me on the face with it.

"You're supposed to be ready."

"You're supposed to be normal."

"Normal bites."

Even though I had fallen for the oldest trick in the book, I was relieved. The storm tide had ebbed. The weirdness that had plagued us had gone back out to sea. The waves were calm again.

Mr. Mora closed his laptop with a click. He had been making some scientific notes and missed everything that had happened between Ty and Bettina.

"I have to say, now that you are all safe and sound and we helped save Willow Key, I'm glad it's all over."

I lifted El Trueno's sword. "But it's not."

ELLISTOWN AIRPORT

All of our parents were waiting for us when the PBY landed. Mr. Mora had called Shelby's parents, Mr. and Mrs. Ruiz, on the Sat phone. Within five minutes all the rest of the parents had heard the entire story. Our parents were *overjoyed* to see us but they were also *angry*. I think they were angry because they found out about all the danger we were in AFTER it all took place. Parents are often illogical like that.

The second we got off the plane, all our parents began speaking at once. Even though they could see that we were all right, they couldn't stop worrying. None of us even got to finish answering their questions.

Mrs. Kolbacher was hugging Wyatt while Mr. Kolbacher was getting on his case. "You took uncertified divers on a *decompression dive*?"

"At one atmosphere, and—"

Mr. Bonglukiet said something in Thai to Din and

Nar. The only words I could pick out were "Coast Guard."

Din started to say something back but didn't get a chance to finish, because my dad said to me, "Mr. Mora broke his ankle and you asked him to *stay*?"

"Only because—"

Mrs. Ruiz said to Shelby, "You were chased by *poachers*?"

"Yeah, but—"

Mr. Conroy said to Bettina, "You fought with *polluters*?"

Bettina said, "Actually, the polluters *were* the poachers and—"

Even Mr. Dyminczyk had taken time off work. He said something to Ty in their language. I had no idea what he said, but he seemed as ultra-upset as the rest of the parents.

Ty is tough to read, but whatever his father said to him didn't seem to tense him out. Ty was standing on an airport tarmac with a group of his closest friends, and that's really all he cared about. He was happy to be wherever the Outriders were.

Then Mr. Dyminczyk stopped speaking and all of the parental haranguing stopped. The crowd on the tarmac parted. Mr. Thorpe, using his aluminum canes, clomped into the center of the turmoil. He ended up next to Mr. Mora who was also holding himself up with crutches. Mr. Thorpe looked down at Mr. Mora's aluminum supports.

"Aren't they dreadful?"

"Hate them," Mr. Mora said.

Then Mr. Thorpe addressed the group. I imagined that he had spoken in front of large crowds before; it seemed easy for him.

"I was never fortunate enough to have children of my own," Mr. Thorpe said, "but I imagine I would be overjoyed if my children returned home healthy, safe, and having helped rescue a protected wilderness area."

My father was not intimidated by Mr. Thorpe's sudden arrival. "My son didn't listen to the Coast Guard! He has to be grounded and grounded hard."

"I agree, William. They all took too many risks and didn't listen to authority."

My father rocked back on his heels for a millisecond. He had no idea that Mr. Thorpe knew his name.

"I think that's why they'll make interesting adults, don't you?" said Mr. Thorpe.

He glanced down at long duffel bag at my feet. I

think he knew that El Trueno's sword was in it. Mr. Thorpe then motioned to a deluxe black van that was idling behind his limousine. He spoke directly to my father.

"Your son and his friends are helping me solve a mystery. I will return them to you before supper when the 'hard grounding' can begin. Is that acceptable?"

My father was swimming way out of his depth, but nodded as if he were a corporate CEO. "Agreed."

BACK AT FALCON'S LAIR

"La columna!" Mr. Thorpe said as he examined the three diamond shaped holes in the sword's blade. "Dona Juliana was said to have been an educated and brilliant woman, and it took another such woman to locate El Trueno's sword," Mr. Thorpe said, now looking directly at Shelby.

I couldn't be sure, but Shelby looked like she was blushing. That's not Shelby-like at all. "Team effort," was all she said.

Mr. Thorpe's butler dude, Giorgio, had laid out a tremendous spread of food and desserts in Mr. Thorpe's solarium. We had all been on the plane for so long without eating, it was hard not to gorge ourselves. Din and Nar are small, but they can consume twice their body weight in food (especially sugar-based items). I even noticed several varieties of pizza. I didn't want Mr. Thorpe to be insulted, so I ate about seven slices, just to be polite. It was the best pizza I've ever tasted.

Giorgio took a big hunk of roast beef, put it on a china plate, and lowered it carefully to the oriental carpeting. Howie, who had been permitted inside the mansion, looked up at Nar. Nar nodded. In one *GLUMPH*, the beef was gone. Howie then made himself comfortable.

We all watched as Mr. Thorpe dipped a rag in some type of solvent and then rubbed it on the blade of El Trueno's sword. Not only was the sword a possible clue to buried treasure, it had saved our lives near the aquifer and been used to do battle with a heinous poacher. It had also almost been used to stab me, but I tried not to think about that.

The solvent dissolved the dull rust on the sword. The blade was now shining like silver. It gleamed in the sunlight that poured through the solarium windows. This must have been what the sword had looked like in El Trueno's day. The steel reflected light all around the room. It was one of those cool moments you spend your life dreaming about, but don't often happen.

Mr. Thorpe put the sword under a magnifying lens. A smile appeared on his lips.

"Look, above these three diamond-shaped holes. Lettering."

We all crowded around to see. Over the first diamond near the hilt there was an *O*. The middle hole had an *R*. And the last diamond, near the tip, had another *O*.

Shelby's eyes lit up. "*Oro!* GOLD!"

Wyatt bent over the magnifying lens and looked closely at the letters. "That is so cool, but what does it mean?"

Mr. Thorpe pulled out the ultra-old map fragment that was laminated in plastic. "Take a look at this." Mr. Thorpe pointed a long, bony finger at a location on the map. The spot where he was pointing would be about one mile north of what is now Sternmetz Marina deep inside Pine Hollow State Forest. For some reason there was a *diamond* drawn on the map where Mr. Thorpe was pointing.

Without saying a word, Mr. Thorpe put the map down on his massive desk and then laid the sword on top of it. He then positioned the diamond hole nearest the hilt directly over the diamond shape on the map. They were exactly the same size! Mr. Thorpe angled the sword so that the diamond-shaped hole lined up perfectly with the diamond drawn on the map. The sword then pointed in a north/south direction.

"We found the treasure!" Bettina thrust her fist into the air.

"I don't think so," I said

"Look, the diamonds match up," Din said.

"But there are *two other holes* in the sword. We're missing the rest of the map. Any of those three holes could match up with that diamond."

Shelby gently picked up the sword and turned it to face the opposite direction. The diamond near the *tip* also matched up perfectly with the diamond on the map. "The sword might face this way. We won't know unless we get more information."

Mr. Thorpe seemed to be watching all of us carefully. I couldn't guess what was going through his mind. Maybe he already knew where the treasure was, or maybe he was just amused by our pitiful attempts to figure out the mystery. It is possible he had just been using us to get the sword and had no intention of including us in the actual treasure hunt. I hoped that wasn't the case, but you can never be sure about Mr. Thorpe. He's not just one move ahead in the chess game; he already has you in checkmate—you just aren't aware of it.

"Also, we don't know if the sword *points* to the location of the treasure, or if it is just part of an even larger puzzle." I looked around and saw that my friends could see the logic in what I had said but were frustrated. They wanted the answer right at this moment—and so did I.

Mr. Thorpe lifted his lips in that sneer-smile of his. "I've spent forty-five years trying to solve this mystery. I guess I'll just have to wait a little longer."

"But you'll solve it, right?" Nar said before taking a humongous bite out of a doughnut.

"I hope so."

"It's just so . . . *frustrating*," I said.

Mr. Thorpe opened a drawer of his desk and pulled out the ancient leather-bound book that was the ship's log of *L'Esperanza*. "You want to know the last words El Trueno ever wrote?" Mr. Thorpe opened the ship's log to the last page. "Shelby?"

Shelby pushed her hair behind her ears and leaned over the book. She read the Spanish, "*¡Diviértase en la búsqueda!*" A smile crept across her lips.

"Translation?" I said.

"'Enjoy the chase!'"

My friends and I had helped bring a poacher/polluter to justice, and we had contributed to a breakthrough scientific discovery that may help save a protected wilderness, but, in the end, we did not locate a centuries-old buried treasure. Alvaro Bautista di Salamanca, better known as the notorious pirate El Trueno, was not giving up his secret so easily. We'd have to wait for our next expedition, Expedition to Pine Hollow, to get more clues.

But that's a whole other story. . . .

TURN THE PAGE FOR A SNEAK PEEK AT THE
OUTRIDERS' NEXT ADVENTURE. . . .

EXPEDITION TO PINE HOLLOW

BOARD NOT BORED

EXPEDITION: PINE HOLLOW

Entry by: Cam Walker

Sakemwah Hill is the tallest point in Pine Hollow State Forest. I'm pretty sure that the hill got its name from the Sakemwah Indians, who were the first people to live in the area around my hometown of Surf Island. Not a whole lot is known about the Sakemwah. Miss Renape, our history teacher at Surf Island Middle School, told us that early explorers wrote about encounters with the Sakemwah and then the whole tribe just seemed to have disappeared.

If you make the four-hour hike to the top of Sakemwah Hill you will find a tower. The tower is about sixteen feet square at the base, and rises to about forty feet. If you picture three sugar cubes stacked on top of each other, that's exactly the shape of the structure. There are three huge mysteries that have never been solved about the tower:

1. No one knows who built it. Was it the Sakem-wah tribe? Was it the early explorers? Was it some long-ago soldiers?
2. The tower is constructed of a light-colored stone that can't be found anywhere on Sakem-wah Hill or in all of Pine Hollow State Forest. Where did the stone come from?
3. There is only one entrance into the tower. It is a narrow opening that is *twenty-five feet above the ground*. The only way to get inside is with a ladder, or with rock-climbing gear (the way we Outriders preferred). What was that about?

Oh, I forgot. There is another strange thing about the tower. There is only ONE decoration on the entire structure. Right above the narrow opening, carved into the light-colored stone, is the image of an eagle, wings outstretched, soaring above Sakem-wah Hill. The tips of the eagle's wings are bent gracefully upward and balanced between them is the fiery orb of the sun.

Right about now you might be wondering why I'm

telling you so much about Eagle Tower (that's what everyone in Surf Island calls it). Eagle Tower is just about the most important place in the world to my friends and me. The first Outrider expedition *ever* was a hike to Eagle Tower. We didn't have any way to climb into the opening, but just making it to the top of Sakemwah Hill was awesome enough. Over the years we've returned to the tower and explored it inside and out. For us, it is kind of like the spot where my friends and I became the Outriders. And now a mining company was going to tear it down.

Somebody—the state legislature, the governor, maybe even the president of the United States—gave permission for this big company to lop off a hunk of Pine Hollow State Forest so that it could dig a humongous open-pit bauxite mine. Mr. Mora, our biology teacher, told us that bauxite is the stuff that aluminum is made of. In about five days, the mining company, Amalgamated Bauxite Industries, was going to start dynamiting all around Eagle Tower. By the time they were through, the tower, Sakemwah Hill, and all of our Outrider memories would be gone.

So you can understand why we had to plan one last expedition into Pine Hollow State Forest. One thing I can say about expeditions is that most times they turn out a lot differently than you planned. For instance, there were a bunch of things we didn't know would happen in Pine Hollow:

1. That we would run into a group of kids from the Bluffs who sort of felt the same way about Eagle Tower as we did;
2. That our friend Bettina was concealing something really important from all of us;
3. That the mining company would start dynamiting five days ahead of schedule.

Oh, I probably should mention that we discovered a lost city and were almost trapped in there for eternity, but you can read all about it in the rest of my blog. . . .